D0906276

The
Deadly Side
of the
Square

Also by Lee Jordan

The Toy Cupboard

The
Deadly Side
of the
Square

Lee Jordan

Walker and Company
New York

First published in the United States of America in 1991
by Walker Publishing Company, Inc., 720 Fifth Avenue,
New York, NY 10019.

Originally published in Great Britain

Library of Congress Cataloging-in-Publication Data
Jordan, Lee.
The deadly side of the square / Lee Jordan.
p. cm.
Originally published: London: Macmillan, 1988.
ISBN 0-8027-5794-4
I. Title
PR6060.06254D4   1991
823'.914--dc20   91-12299
                                                      CIP
Printed in the United States of America

2   4   6   8   10   9   7   5   3   1

1

Sophie Mendel was afraid. She had been afraid in spasms since Maria's body was found and she felt safe only once her front door was closed behind her. Now, as the Number Twenty-four bus made its way through Pimlico towards the Thames, her fears grew. She would have to leave the bus, get out of the warm saloon into the bitter winter air, leave behind the security of the other passengers and the conductor, who swung up and down the stairs like a gibbon she had once watched in the Berlin Zoo.

The bus began to slow. This was her stop. She waited until it had come to a halt, then made her way stiffly along the aisle.

'You all right, lady?' The conductor was a Sikh in a turban.

'Don't start until I get off!' she said severely. Even after all the years she had lived in England, her accent still told of her German background. 'You hear me?'

'I hear you. Whole of Pimlico hears you.'

She let herself down gently onto the pavement.

'Now can we go?' he said, with heavy sarcasm.

Mrs Mendel was impervious. 'Yes. Now you can go.'

The red bus disappeared down the road, leaving her alone.

She walked to a zebra crossing, looked right, looked left, listened intently, then stepped onto the road and hurried across as quickly as she could. There would come a time, she thought, when she would have to depend even more on her ears, for each month it seemed her field of vision grew narrower. She went in the direction of the Southern Railway, where it formed an angle with a Metropolitan Waterboard pumping station. She crossed Inkerman Street and saw the entrance to Sebastopol Square looming up through the mist.

By enveloping houses, shortening vistas and cloaking trees, the mist gave the square a ghostly beauty it did not normally possess. It was a small square by London standards and lying as it did, next to the waste ground of the railway, had not enjoyed the same trendy refurbishment as other parts of Pimlico. As housing grew ever more expensive, this was changing. Several houses had already been done up, but it would take some time yet before the square could be called handsome, as once it had been.

It still looked seedy, uncared for. Under the mist, the plane trees were motionless and the untidy privet hedges which hid the communal gardens were coated with hoar frost. Residents were supposed to be able to use the gardens for their pleasure – there was even a tennis court. Each was supposed to have a key. But the gate hung open on its hinges, the fence was broken and there were holes in the hedge. Once it had been an amenity, but now it was more a dumping ground for old bedsteads and broken chairs. Ask Maria how much of an amenity it was, Sophie thought. Ask her, if you could. That's where they had found her body. The square was cut off, dead, part of a diseased urban landscape.

At one of its corners, next door but one to the house in which Sophie lived, was S. Flower and Son. 'S' stood for Sidney (deceased) and 'Son' stood for Ronnie. 'We stand on a corner and that's what we are, a corner shop,' Ronnie had said to her once. 'Can't get rarer than that nowadays.

That's why we're a little dearer. Convenience. You don't have to go up West, see?'

She did see, and he was right, it *was* convenient. She still didn't like paying a 'convenience' price, but there was no other shop within four blocks and four blocks in mist or rain or when the streets were icy or dark (or, after what had happened to Maria, at *any* time), four blocks were too much.

The shop occupied the ground floor of a double-fronted house with the basement acting as stock-room and the two upper floors partly as store-rooms and partly as dwelling for Mrs Mavis Flower and Ronnie.

Sophie paused as she drew level with the shop door and saw the small figure of an old woman dressed in a dark coat and black hat, with stick-like legs, emerge. She stepped aside for her, and realised she had mistaken her own image in the glass door. The fear of her failing sight was like a palimpsest overlaid by her new fears, but was there, nevertheless. 'You will never go completely blind,' the specialist had said. But how could he be sure? Whose eyes were they?

She did not want to go into the shop because she might spend money and if Stefan had bought her all the things she wanted there was no need. But he had been acting queerly lately. Not to be trusted. This business of wanting to live in the country. This was his new rubbish. Where was he to get the money for that? She shook her head in irritation. Stefan and all his women. His 'ladies', as he called them. She pushed open the shop door. Either the springs were getting stronger or she was getting weaker, because it became more of an effort every time.

Ronnie was unpacking pork pies and displaying them on the counter. You had to be careful where you stepped in S. Flower and Son. She had barked her shin several times on objects she had not seen. Once Stefan had cracked his head on a hanging birdcage and had been dizzy all day. The shop contained a prodigious number of things: milk and newspapers and cigarettes; groceries and birdseed and sometimes even birds. (This was where she had bought Winston.) It sold potatoes and tomatoes and other greengroceries; cheese and bacon and butter, writing pads and postcards and envelopes and get-well cards and birthday cards and modelling kits for aeroplanes and cars and soldiers, and pens and pencils, rubbers, Christmas wrapping paper at Christmas-time, and at any other time for that matter. Its shelves went up to the ceiling. Other goods hung suspended or stood in piles on the floor and the customer had to pick his way between them. Ronnie Flower had been right: it was rare, one of the last of its breed, the corner shop with worn linoleum and milk crates outside the door and an interior that smelled of old luncheon meat and stale cheddar.

Ronnie finished arranging the pork pies tastefully on the wooden counter. He was in his late twenties, large and plump. He sweated a lot, even in winter. He reminded Sophie of the young Liberace and she felt that if she pressed her finger into his cheek it would cause a dimple that might remain. His face wore the habitual expression of a shrewd infant.

'Good morning, Mrs Mendel. How are we today?'

'We ain't so good.' She picked her way towards the counter past an open sack of potatoes that looked to her in the dim light like a crouching beast. 'Miss Krause got, what you say, cremated. That's where I come from. Twenty-four bus all the way.'

She thought of the chapel and the cheap coffin, the soft throb of the organ. It was a record, of course. She was the only mourner. They weren't going to get an organist just for her. How long had she known Maria? Forty years? Once there had been so many of them. Now only she and

Stefan, and she'd known he wouldn't come even before she asked him.

'I don't go to funerals,' he had said. 'When it's my own, yes, then I go.' That was the trouble with Poles, she thought, no responsibility, always women and money and this and that.

'Sad,' Ronnie Flower said. 'A very sad thing.'

'Sad? It's a shocking thing!'

'How's that, then?' He rearranged the pies, balancing them on one another.

'Because of what the police say,' she said indignantly. 'I tell you something for nothing, it wasn't no heart attack. Mugging, more like.'

'They say there was no evidence.'

'And I say the evidence was that she never went into the gardens. Miss Krause? A maiden lady? Never, never. She was afraid. I say they mugged her and dragged her in and stole her money.'

'Who's they?' Ronnie said.

'They is whoever did it.'

'The police say there wasn't a mark on her, except where she fell. She died a natural death. Heart failure. It's coming to us all.'

'What about the money then?'

'Come on, Mrs Mendel! In this area? A handbag, just lying there? You expect no one to touch it?'

Mrs Flower came from the rear of the shop, through an archway which had had to be widened to accommodate her size. She was one of the largest women Sophie had ever seen. She was wearing a floral dress that bulged ominously in places and her upper lip was shadowed by facial hair.

'It's glandular,' Sophie had once said to Stefan.

'She told you that? You believe her, you'll believe anything. I tell you what it is. Waste. That's where that fat comes from.'

9

'Waste?'

'You think they throw away those sausages and those pies? Never.'

'You mean they eat all the things they can't sell?' Disbelief had rung in her voice.

'Why not? It's cheaper that way.'

Now Mrs Flower said, 'Good morning, dear.'

'She's been to Miss Krause's funeral,' Ronnie said.

'Cremation. Twenty-four bus all the way.'

'You were lucky.'

'It's lucky going to a cremation?'

'I mean about the bus.'

Sophie moved nearer the counter, and banged her foot against a box of leeks.

'How are your eyes, dear? Mrs Flower said.

She did not wish to discuss her eyes and instead said crossly, 'How's your fibrositis?'

Mrs Flower raised her eyes to the ceiling and patted her shoulders. 'Ronald rubs them with lanolin. How's Mr Nedza's cough?'

'Terrible. I tell him over and over he must stop smoking cigarettes.'

Mrs Flower's face tightened. The cigarettes were bought in her shop. Sophie pretended not to notice. 'Did he come in? He had a list.'

'I haven't seen him today,' Ronnie said.

She tried to remember what was on the list she had given him.

'I saw him yesterday, though,' Ronnie said. 'He was going into Greeley's.'

Sophie's mind produced a picture of the jewellery shop at the Victoria Station end of the Vauxhall Bridge Road. It was a long walk there and back. Stefan had not told her he was going to Greeley's. He said he was going to see the doctor about his cough. She frowned. She did not like things happening she did not know about.

10

'Buying you a diamond ring?' Ronnie said.

The joke fell flat.

'Maybe he was selling,' Mrs Flower said.

Sophie knew that was unlikely. She wondered if he was becoming senile. This talk of living in the country. But that was something she was not going to discuss with the Flowers. Her attention returned to the list. There hadn't been much on it, or at least not much that she could recall. She ordered a few items, then remembered something else. 'Oh, yes, and birdseed.'

'How is he, dear?'

'He don't like the cold.'

'Who does?' Mrs Flower moved one of her shoulders.

Sophie took out her purse and tried to see what money there was; one pound coins were the hardest to identify. As she was paying, the door opened with a shrill ringing of its bell. When Ronnie spoke, his voice was so harsh that she started.

'Out!' he said. 'I told you before. You want to come in here, you come in one at a time.'

She turned. Four young boys had come into the shop. She found ages difficult to guess now, but they couldn't have been more than thirteen or fourteen. The same age as Leni when she died. Their heads were shaven, apart from a fringe of hair in front, and they wore sleeveless T-shirts, rolled-up jeans with braces, and heavy Doc Martins. They did not seem to feel the cold. Their aggression was palpable. They stood in silence, looking at Ronnie. Then the one at the front, slightly bigger than the others, with the beginnings of a moustache and cold grey eyes, moved his head slightly and the three behind him left the shop. They did not seem cowed or even sullen, but left a feeling of coldness.

'Didn't you see the notice on the door?' Ronnie said.

'Yeah.'

11

'I'm not fooling. You come in here one at a time or you don't come in at all.'

Mrs Flower was watching out of the corner of her eye as she handed Sophie her change.

'You try to keep a decent shop,' she said. 'It's hardly worth it any more.'

Sophie took her purchases and turned away. The boy was going through boxes of model aircraft on one of the shelves. Ronnie was watching him closely. Sophie opened the door.

'You been to Spain?' Mrs Flower said. 'Costa del Sol?'

'No,' Sophie said. Outside the shop, she hurried past the three boys, who stood in a semi-circle on the pavement. The mist seemed thicker now. As she went along the side of Sebastopol Square it was as though she had cut herself off from the movements and the sounds of London.

She heard a kind of scraping noise behind her. A footstep, perhaps. Her old heart gave a jerk and she felt her hands and feet become blocks of ice. On her left was the decaying garden, the rusty stop-netting on the tennis court, torn and broken. This was where Maria had been found.

'Come now,' she said to herself in German. 'Be a brave girl.'

The words were her father's. There was a flash of memory and she was on the beach near Lübeck. The waves had been high that day and she had been afraid. He had held her under the arms and lifted her as each wave came in. My God, when was that? It must have been nearly seventy years ago.

A car turned into the square. She stood on the pavement watching it park. A man got out, slammed the door and went into one of the houses. There *were* other people, she thought. She was not alone. Gathering her courage, she turned to look behind her, but all she could see was the mist and other parked cars looking like monoliths. Nothing moved now. She went on. She had not felt afraid in the streets like this since Berlin in its last days, just before it had finally fallen to the Russians. There had been several hours when all firing had ceased, when the city had gone quiet. Then the tanks had arrived.

She was getting close now. She felt for her key. Then she heard the footsteps again, quite clearly this time, and more than one person. She thought of the shaven heads and the braces, the heavy boots. She tried to hurry, but feared she might slip. God knew what would happen then. A broken hip, and into Pimlico House. They'd take her whether she wanted to go or not. And once in there . . .

The footsteps came near. But now her hand was on the basement rail of her own flat. She opened the old black iron gate and felt her way down to her doorway. The footsteps stopped. Maybe they were watching her. She managed to get the key into the lock, and opened her door, then slammed it defiantly behind her. She put up the chain and double-locked it. She leaned against it, getting her breath. She was home. She was safe.

She took off her coat and hat and put them away, then she went into the little kitchen and put away her groceries.

She had forgotten the ritual she and Maria Krause and Stefan Nedza had conducted for years with almost religious fervour: the coming-home signals. These had started when they'd had to admit to each other that they were no longer young. By that time, Miss Krause was the only tenant left in the house next door and she and Stefan were the only ones in her house.

Maria Krause had lived in the basement on the other side of Sophie's own wall and they had been able to communicate through a locked double door that had once joined the basement apartments when the houses had been a single entity. They had evolved a series of signals like prisoners in a gaol so that they could attract each

13

other's attention to say when they were going out, then used the old wartime V for Victory, dot–dot–dot–dash, to say they were safely home. She had a different system with Stefan. They were on a shared telephone line, and some years before when a telephone engineer had come to sort out a fault she had watched him dial a number and heard her own telephone ring. He had told her that each household had a secret number which would ring its own phone so that engineers could test the line. She had wheedled the number out of him and ever since had used it to communicate with Stefan's extension. You dialled, you heard an engaged signal, you put the receiver down and it started to ring. Simple. She dialled it now. It rang and rang. She waited.

'Where is he?' she said, addressing Winston, the light green budgie that perched in its cage at the end of the room. It gripped one of the cage bars with its beak and twisted its head, looking at her.

'Why didn't he tell me he was going out?' *Warum?*' She was aware that now, with age, she mixed up English and German just as Stefan mixed Polish with whatever he was saying.

'Talk English!' she would say, putting her hands over her ears. 'I don't understand that language.'

'Polish! It's Polish!'

'It hurts my ears. You live in England. Speak English!'

'Shall I go up now and see?' she said to the budgerigar.

But she was exhausted. Her legs felt like rhubarb. A few minutes rest and then she could face the stairs.

'A minute. Two minutes. Then I go up.' She sat down in her armchair.

Winston turned upside-down, then righted himself and defecated accurately into his water.

2

The voice was like a flood-tide, rising and falling, but always rising more than it fell; there was something remorseless, inexorable about it. 'Here,' Mrs Flower was saying, indicating her left shoulder. 'And then lower down. In the middle of my back. And my knees are something dreadful, especially with all the standing. Well, I mean, you got to stand in a shop. And lifting. That's another thing. I can't lift things no more. Here . . .' She indicated her bottom. 'Like hot knives.'

Dr Margaret Hollis stared past her. It had been a long, hard day, but Mrs Flower was her last patient. She dominated the surgery, making it seem smaller than it really was. Maggie's thoughts were on her immediate future. She wasn't on duty tonight. That was the best thought. A hot bath. A strong drink. Maybe two, or a glass of wine with her meal. And she would cook something nice, not just open a tin or a packet. It had been a long time since she had sat down by herself to a meal of her own cooking, a proper meal.

'Makes me dizzy,' Mrs Flower was saying. 'It's pressure, like. In the right one . . .'

As far as she could remember, there was nothing in the fridge, but the delicatessen didn't close until nine and the supermarket until eleven. She had a choice. What about Chinese? That was relatively easy and she would be able to get all the ingredients at the supermarket. Lemon chicken? She'd need a couple of chicken breasts, spring onions, she had lemons. Light soy and dark soy. Sesame oil. She supposed she still had those. God, how long had it been? She hadn't cooked Chinese since Alec died. Did soy go off? It couldn't. Nor could sesame oil. If she bought some frozen broccoli she could make broccoli with ginger. And a bottle of cold white wine. And then . . . maybe she'd spoil herself and watch television. She hadn't watched any for some time. It had been like a drug at the beginning and she'd had to tell herself it could be as bad as any other. So she had started reading again.

'Spain.' Mrs Flower was looking at her with raised eyebrows. 'Have you been to the Costa del Sol?' Maggie stared at the gross woman who came to see her as a private patient at least twice a month. 'That's where Ronald wants to go for his holiday. Somewhere near Torremolinos, he says. I say what about me? I don't trust them doctors. I'm not putting one foot out of Sebastopol Square. Anyway, I like me own bed.'

Maggie had inherited her from Alec. Her notes were two inches thick. She had been to every endocrinologist, cardiologist, physiologist, every ENT man, at the two nearest teaching hospitals. When she had first come to Maggie complaining about shortness of breath and pains in her joints, Maggie had tried with some tact to suggest that she eat less.

'It's glandular,' Mrs Flower had said indignantly.

'No, it's not,' Maggie had said. 'It doesn't say anything about that in your notes.'

'Your husband said it was glandular.'

'I don't think so, Mrs Flower.'

She had left then, full of anger. But a fortnight later she was back. Something else was wrong: another muscle, another joint, the back of her head, her calves, stomach, colon, liver, kidneys.

' . . . years. I mean, he's got brochures for everywhere.

16

But it's Spain, he says. Well, I say, not in *my* state of health.'

Maggie wrote out a prescription for her usual placebo.

'Thank you, doctor. Couldn't live without these.'

Maggie watched her huge backside go out of the door. It reminded her of the Lipizzaners she had seen at the Spanish Riding School in Vienna, the great, rounded haunches driving the heavy back legs.

She flicked the intercom and told her receptionist, Mrs Castle, that she could go home. Then she sat back, stretching in her chair. This had always been the best time with Alec. Odd that the roles should be so completely reversed. It was he who would have been sitting here, she in the flat upstairs waiting for him, looking forward to his off-duty night. They were the nights they made love, starting just after dinner, sometimes even before. They would drink a bottle of claret and Alec would smoke a cigar. 'Don't tell anyone,' he had once said, smiling. 'But a little of what you fancy . . .'

She felt a momentary constriction of her throat. Don't be so bloody maudlin, she said to herself.

It was nearly seven o'clock and the winter's night had long since closed down on London. She put out her light and opened the long curtains, letting in the lights of Balaclava Place. Then she went through her reception-room on her way to the stairs and the top three floors of the house. Someone was sitting in one of the chairs.

'Kenneth!' she said.

He rose. 'You sound surprised.'

'Of course not. You startled me, that's all.'

He was tall and thin, with an angular face, and expensively dressed in a dark business suit. He had a bunch of early, forced daffodils in his hand and said, 'For you.'

She was touched. 'They're beautiful. God, don't they just say "spring"!'

'Hungry?'

17

'Starving.'

'Shall we eat now or later?'

She'd forgotten her date. She was never on duty on a Thursday evening, so it had become a regular thing, but having forgotten she wasn't mentally prepared. Dinner and a glass or two of wine would change that, she'd be more relaxed. She thought of the lemon chicken. She could make it for him. But her mind rejected the idea instantly. Going to bed with him was one thing, it released tensions that needed releasing. But to sit with him, to cook for him, to eat and laugh and talk with him in her own surroundings as she had with Alec – somehow that was too intimate.

'Let's eat now,' she said. 'Give me a minute and I'll put these in water.'

They went to a trattoria in Lower Sloane Street. The yellow awning, the bright, coloured lights, the raffia-covered *fiascos*, the vine leaves and the netting, all did their best to cheer up the cold, misty night. They ate white-bait and then had cannelloni as a main dish and drank a bottle of Barolo between them. He talked about his daughter, Joan. He was hoping to get her into St Paul's.

'... every term,' he was saying, 'I mean, when inflation's standing at five per cent the fees go up by seven. If it's running at ten, they hit you for fifteen.'

She tried to concentrate, nodding and making sympathetic noises. She watched him as he ate his cannelloni.

She had met Kenneth Deacon when she remodelled the top floor of her house as a self-contained flat. He owned an estate agency in Belgrave Road and she had put the letting of it into his hands. They had discovered a mutual bond when he had first come to see it. He had lost his wife at about the same time as she had lost Alec. She was feeling very raw still and she knew what it must be like for him: the people they both loved had been taken

18

from them suddenly; they'd had no time to get used to the dying. He had been kind and gentle and understanding and he was an attractive man physically. In a way it had been a small miracle. She could have been left in her numb cocoon: lonely and bitter. Instead she had found Kenneth and she was grateful.

She knew he had a house in Prince's Square, but she had never been there because of his daughter.

'. . . to Austria,' he was saying. 'I want her to learn while she's young. I never did and I'm too old to start. I'd be scared stiff of breaking a leg. Did you ever ski?'

'Once,' she said. 'In France. The snow was either too hard or too soft or too wet or too dry. I think I was just unlucky.'

'The school's doing a package, but it's going to be at least six hundred if you include the cost of ski-hire.'

Kenneth talked about money a great deal. Still, she supposed, if you were in business that was what you were in business for. And school fees must be horrendous. But she wouldn't have minded how much they cost. She envied him. She would have given anything to have a daughter of her own. Kenneth's love for Joan was one of his most attractive characteristics.

'What do you think?' he said.

She had not been listening, and hesitated.

She saw a flash of irritation in his eyes. 'I was talking about the Isle of Wight. When Joan is skiing. We could get a weekend if you were free.'

She had been with him once to an expensive hotel near Ventnor. He had talked about the future. He seemed to assume that when Joan was a little older he and Maggie would marry. He had taken her to the cliffs near Bonchurch and shown her a stone-built house with a wide verandah and a magnificent view out over the sea, and said he would buy a place like that and they would come down every weekend. He said there was

19

an exclusive golf-club nearby and he was angling to get his name down for membership. Later they had walked round the dull, provincial streets of the seaside town in autumn and something inside her had quailed. Was that really to be her future? Golf with Kenneth at Ventnor?

He called for the bill and she watched as he added up each item. Then he nodded. She breathed freely. Sometimes he found little mistakes and there would be an argument.

They went back to her flat above the surgery. She felt good in the car. It was a new BMW and had the marvellous new-car smell she had almost forgotten. In the flat she noticed the flowers again and she turned to him and said, 'They're lovely Kenneth.'

'So are you.'

She smiled and put out her hand and he took it. 'Drink? More coffee?'

'Not now. Maybe later.'

She lay in the bed feeling him moving on top of her. As always the initial reaction was one of slight revulsion but she knew this was her fault and told herself that it would eventually disappear as time blurred Alec's absence. But she also knew that her need was strong and she reached up and put her arms about him and held him tightly and pretended he was Alec. He moved his head to kiss her but she turned away and put her cheek against his.

When it was over she lay in the dark, staring at nothing, feeling drained, empty. At that moment the telephone rang.

3

Sophie woke suddenly, deathly cold and quite stiff.
The table light was on but now night had come and the
light's penumbra was too dark for her eyes to penetrate.
She could see shapes, but that was about all. Her two
armchairs faced what had once been the open fireplace,
but which was now a gas fire. Behind her was the table
on which she had her meals. There was a glass-fronted
sideboard containing several plates that her husband had
once said were Chinese, and valuable, and several porce-
lain mugs that he had bought during Royal coronations
and jubilees. There was an old bakelite radio and a small
black and white television set, a bookcase containing a
number of magazines. Above the fireplace there were
three photographs in oval frames. The first showed a
young soldier in German uniform, the second a man in
his sixties, dressed in his Sunday best. Between them was
a photograph of a young girl turning towards the camera.
She had dark, plaited hair and was laughing. She was about
eleven years old.

Sophie's eyes could see none of these things clearly.
Even the other chair looked like a dark rock or a
tree-stump. She struggled upright and began to hunt for
matches to light the gas fire. The flat was freezing. She
found a box in the kitchen and the glow of the fire gave
not only warmth, but a certain cheerfulness. She stopped
suddenly, listening. The noise came again: a scratching.

She knew what it was; it was the dog from a couple of houses along. It was after her dustbins. But she remembered putting the lids on firmly.

The flat consisted of this one room, a bedroom that let off it, the kitchen and a tiny bathroom. The gas fire was the only warmth.

Then she remembered: the cremation, the fearful walk home, the food, shopping . . . and Stefan. She picked up her phone, dialled, but it just went on ringing and ringing.

'Where is he?' she said to Winston. The budgerigar pecked at its reflection in a small mirror. She recalled that she had been about to check Stefan's flat before she had fallen asleep. Mostly she slept in cat-naps, but sometimes after an occasion like Maria's cremation, which had drained her of both physical and mental strength, she would sleep like a sick animal until some of her vitality was restored.

'Now I must go,' she said to the budgie.

She heard the dog scratching at the rubbish bins again. 'Get away!' she called. 'Raus! Raus!'

She took a heavy torch and went into her kitchen. What looked like a long cupboard stood against the far wall. She opened its door and disclosed a small wooden staircase. Once, when such lives were still lived, it had been the servants' entry from the old kitchen into the house itself. Now she mounted it, took down a key which hung from a hook on the inside of the door at the top, unlocked it, and let herself into the ground floor.

It was cold, dark and quiet. She switched on the powerful torch that Maria had given her for her birthday two years previously.

Lily Oppenheimer had once lived in a flat on the ground floor. It had been carved out of one big room. The walls were only plasterboard, so thin that if you stood near the front door you could hear Lily coughing. Poor Lily. Last

22

time Sophie had seen her had been in Pimlico House, just before she had been banished to the fifth floor. She had been sitting in a corner of the lounge, withdrawn, not speaking, endlessly leafing through her bank book and mumbling to herself about the money. That is what Sophie feared most: ending up like Lily.

Once you could no longer look after yourself, once you became too sick or too senile, they took you up to the fifth floor and there was no return from there: just a bed, and the only thing that was your own was your nightdress; everything else, all your little prized possessions, had to go.

Lily was not the only one who had once lived in the house. There was a time when this and the adjoining house had been full. Wilhelm had also gone to Pimlico House; now he was only ashes in an urn. Friedrich had once lived above Stefan, but the stairs had become too much for him and he had moved away; she did not know where. And there had been Eva and her husband – what was his name? Carl. Eva and Carl. They had had a maisonette in the house Maria lived in but in the bitter winter a few years ago they had stuffed up the cracks in the windows to stop the draughts coming in and then had left the kerosene heater burning. No one had gone up to see them for more than twenty-four hours, and they had slowly asphyxiated.

Now only Stefan and herself were left in this house, the other was empty.

She climbed the stairs to the first floor. You'd think that for all the shortage of accommodation in London, new people would have moved in as soon as a flat became empty. But that wasn't the case. The windows had been covered up and the doors padlocked in case of squatters. She wasn't even sure now who owned the house. She had once put it to Mr Ringham when he came for the rent but he denied that he was the owner and said something about a property company. She didn't know whether to believe him or not. Still, she didn't care who owned it. They were safe. No one could force them to leave. Except . . . except if they couldn't look after themselves. And then it would be Pimlico House, and the threat of the fifth floor.

She reached Stefan's flat and paused to get her breath, then felt for the key above the architrave of his door. They had an agreement that he would leave a key where she could reach it, just in case. Their lives now were filled with anticipating situations they placed under a broad heading of 'just in case'.

She opened the door and went in. The flat was in darkness and she had to steel herself to put on the light in case her worst fears were realised. It was a one-roomed flat. The room was large and had two sash windows that looked out onto the backyard. He had turned it into a bedsitter with a small kitchen and smaller bathroom. She could smell him. It was the pomade he used on his hair. The room reeked of it. He was vain about his hair. Although it was white, he still had a full head. Otherwise there was no sign of him.

She peered into the bathroom and the kitchen. All was neat, for he was a very neat man. It was one of the strengths he had with his ladies. He gave them no problems in that way. He did not ask to be looked after like a child. Lily had told her that. Lily had probably had an affair with him in the old days. She had never spoken of it, but how would you know a thing like that about a man unless from personal experience?

She put out the light, locked the door, replaced the key and retraced her steps to her own flat, locking the communicating door as she did so. She went into the sitting-room, which had warmed up. 'That's better,' she said to Winston. 'That's much better.' She held her hands towards the fire. Then she heard the dog again. She went to the door and shouted, 'Raus! Raus!' Usually her voice frightened it away, but not this time. She fetched a broom from the kitchen, opened the door on the chain, poked the broom outside, and banged it against the wall. There was no sudden scurry as the dog leapt up the basement steps to the street. Instead the scratching, grating noise continued. She reached for her torch and poked it through the door. The first thing she saw was water dripping down the area steps. 'My God,' she said out loud. 'A broken pipe. In the morning that will be ice.'

She raised the torch beam. It played on a man's face. He was upside down, lying sprawled on the steps. The water was blood which was flowing from his head. One of his legs was twitching and his shoe was scratching and scraping against the railing.

'Oh God!' Terror gripped her throat. 'Stefan!'

She opened the door and went to him. He must have slipped and fallen. She could feel the slight fluttering of his breath but she did not have the strength to move him. She went back into her flat. She was trembling and confused, but she knew she had to phone someone. A doctor. He went to the same panel of doctors as she did. She dialled. Her call was routed to a switchboard that relayed a recorded message. She tried to speak to the recording but it kept on saying the same thing: that the doctor was on call but would be back in a few minutes. Would she please leave a message after the tone.

'What tone?' she asked. 'What is tone?'

'Dr Rankin is on call,' the voice repeated. 'He will be back in a short while. Please leave a message after the tone and he will get back to you.'

She put down the receiver and picked up her little telephone book. She dialled the private number of her own doctor, Dr Hollis.

4

The man who stood on the front step of Maggie Hollis's house was big. His body blocked out the street-lights, but the light from her own front hall illuminated him. He held a small piece of paper in his hand. On the step beside him was a Lark suiter. A black flight-bag was slung on his shoulder.

'Good evening,' he said. 'Dr Hollis?'

'Yes, but I'm afraid evening surgery is over. This is my private entrance.'

He said, 'No. I'm quite well, thank you.' The accent was American, soft and unexaggerated. He glanced at his piece of paper and then at the number above the door. 'I've come about the apartment.'

'It's rather late. Didn't the estate agent . . .?'

'They said between two and four.' He consulted his watch. 'I guess it is late.'

She looked at him more closely. He was about thirty-five, wearing a mackintosh and a heavy scarf. His face was big and square and lightly dotted with freckles. His hair was sandy. He looked, she thought, like a single-handed yachtsman, a part of the outdoors.

'I waited in for you,' she said.

'I owe you an apology, but my flight only got in at noon and there was something I had to do first.'

'I have my rounds now, so perhaps tomorrow . . . I'll be in about lunchtime . . .'

'I'll take it.'

'Take what?'

'The apartment.'

'But you haven't seen it!'

He smiled. 'That's because you won't show it to me.'

'I told you. I have patients to see. And anyway . . .'

He pointed over his shoulder. 'I saw an Italian restaurant a couple of blocks back. I'll eat while you're seeing your patients. I'll come back, then you can show it to me. How's that?'

'I think it would be much better if you came back tomorrow.'

'Ma'am, the agency said you wanted your tenant to be a visitor to England. I'm a visitor.'

'How long would you want it for?'

'Two, three months.'

She was tempted. 'I usually let for six.'

'Okay. But can't we discuss it?'

'Oh, all right. They did give me your name, but I've . . .'

'Seago. Bill Seago.'

'Well, you go and have your dinner, Mr Seago. I'll be back in an hour or so.'

'I appreciate it.' He picked up the suitcase as though it contained cotton wool and turned to go down the steps.

'Try the prosciutto,' she said. 'It's good.'

'Thank you. I'll do that.'

She watched him from the window as he walked along Balaclava Place. Three or four young skinheads were coming towards Sebastopol Square on the same side of the street. She found herself holding her breath, then they stepped off the pavement into the street and Seago continued on his way. The boys paused, turned and stared after him. He seemed oblivious of them. She watched him until he crossed Inkerman Street and disappeared from view. The boys, too, had vanished. There

27

had been some rain earlier and the black streets glistened under the sodium lights. She stood there for several minutes, lost in thought. What she had seen was like a sudden glimpse of the jungle: the big predator moving unconcerned through the territory of lesser animals. The problem was that he did not know how dangerous these lesser creatures could be once they formed a pack. She shivered. She herself had never been touched, nor had her car. Was it that doctors and midwives were immune? Or had she simply been lucky? She thought of the old man lying on the basement steps, blood pouring from a gash in his head. There had been ice on the pavement where a milk bottle had broken, so the likelihood was that he had slipped. But . . . No one could be sure. Old Mrs Mendel was certain that he had been mugged, but she had said that about Miss Krause as well. In this part of London old people were terrified of being mugged and the tragedy was that it meant they viewed all young people with suspicion, thereby increasing the hostility between youth and age, exacerbating the generation gap. But old people *were* mugged and they *were* terrified. Sometimes she was afraid herself. She glanced around at the special locks on the windows, the heavy chain on her front door. Defensible space, the architects called it. Not home, or Chez Nous or Dunromin, but defensible space.

She shrugged into a camel-hair coat, picked up her medical bag and went out into the cold night, double-locking the door behind her. Her car was parked a few paces up the road: small, French and cheap. It didn't do to have an expensive car in London any more, especially if you left it in the street. As she passed the mouth of Sebastopol Square she saw the skinheads. They were standing near the broken gate in a group. Then they went into the gardens, making for the old tennis hut, which was now an empty shell.

As she did the round of her bedridden patients, Pimlico began to settle down for the night. Along the Embankment the traffic was still heavy, but in the maze of one-way streets that criss-crossed what had, in the nineteenth century, been London's market garden, there were few cars.

The 'Crimea', as it was called locally, was more than half a mile from the bright lights of any restaurants. Here people closed up their houses early, checked the deadlocks and the chains, the bolts and the mortices. They watched television, but always with part of their hearing tuned, like a wild animal's, to sounds that did not fit into the pattern: a sliding window, a footstep, a creaking staircase, an opening door.

Mrs Flower and Ronald had closed up the shop for the night. Ronald had put out the empty milk crates and brought in the boxes of green vegetables that sat out under an awning during shop hours.

In the kitchen behind the shop Mrs Flower had made a hot-pot of bacon ends, frankfurters and pieces of pork luncheon meat whose sell-by dates had slipped quietly into history but which could not be thrown away – at least, not while she was the housekeeper.

'Have a little more, Ronald.' She scooped up a frankfurter and a dumpling that she had made from stale white bread. 'And you're not going to leave your potato, are you?'

Ronnie ate without tasting. Quantity was his criterion. There was a pile of brochures on the table in front of him. 'Here's one,' he said, pushing a single sheet over the plastic tablecloth. 'Look at that.' It showed blue skies and empty beaches.

'You still on about Spain?' She ladled another spoonful of hot-pot onto his plate. 'What about Bournemouth? There's some lovely places down there.'

'That's the Costa bloody Geriatrica, not the Costa del Sol.'

'Don't use words like that at table! Your father wouldn't have it, and I won't, either.'

'Okay, okay.'

'What do you say?'

'Sorry. Happy? Satisfied?' He rose.

'Where you going?'

'I got to see someone.'

'What about all this?' She indicated the table.

'Oh, Christ! Sorry, sorry . . . okay, let's get moving then.'

'Don't you want your pudding?' It was tinned marmalade sponge.

'I'll have it later.' He began to collect the plates and carry them to the sink. He helped her to wash up, then went down into the shop. He took a package from one of the shelves and let himself out into the winter cold.

In Sebastopol Square Sophie Mendel was listening. Her ears were like sensitive hydrophones. They had become even more so since her eyesight had begun to fail. It was as though she was compensating for the weakening of one sense with the strengthening of another. 'You're lucky!' she told herself more than once when depression hit her. What if they were both to go? And, at her age, why shouldn't they?

The sounds came from the gardens across the way. A sudden burst of laughter, a shout, footsteps on gravel. But from her basement she could see nothing of the street outside unless she went out and climbed the steps to the pavement; the steps down which they said Stefan had slipped. She thought of him lying in hospital with tubes up his nose, his eyes flickering open every now and then, the bandages that enclosed his head. A slip! Rubbish! One day he would wake up and tell them and she knew she would be vindicated. No, she would not go up the steps.

30

But it was part of Sophie's survival kit to know what was going on around her. Knowledge gave her the chance of adapting and she knew that above everything she must adapt to circumstances.

She tried watching the television to take her mind away from the voices but found herself uneasy, for the noise of the programmes masked what might be happening in the world outside her door. She switched it off and listened again. She thought it might be starting to rain. If that were so it would drive them out of the gardens – whoever they were – for the old tennis hut had no roof. If only she could see the street, see them come out of the gardens and go away, then she could settle for the night.

Then she remembered the inner staircase. She reached for her torch and went up onto the ground floor. Two narrow windows on either side of the front door had been boarded up. The flats had had corrugated-iron placed over their windows. She thought of the letter-box. The flap had never closed properly and someone, long ago, had ripped it off and thrown it away because it had banged in the wind. She knelt by the door, letting herself down slowly onto her knees. A street-light gave her a good view of the broken gate and the gardens beyond.

At that moment she saw a figure move quickly along the pavement and enter the gate. She had the impression of a big man. She turned her head and put her ear to the letter-box and heard the voices again. Then another voice, lower, deeper. Then silence. She watched for several more minutes but all she could see was an urban wasteland brilliantly illuminated by an orange light. Her knees were aching and she decided she had done enough spying for one night. As she moved to straighten up she touched an envelope on the doormat. Probably a circular for Stefan or even for Lily – they still arrived after more than a year – telling her that she had been selected to enter some great competition with enormous prizes. She tucked it into the pocket of her apron, locked her door at the top of her little staircase and went down to her sitting-room.

She stood still for a moment, listening, but she no longer heard the voices; instead she heard the sounds of the house all around her. Once she and Morris had taken a cottage in Wales for their summer holidays and she had woken up on the first night and heard noises and felt afraid, thinking of ghosts or murderers, Bluebeard, perhaps, until she had frightened herself into such a state that she had wakened him and made him listen with her and then he had told her that old houses did creak in the night, that boards contracted or expanded, water ran through pipes, tanks filled and grew heavy; that creakings and groanings were normal. And he had gone back to sleep and left her and she had listened to the noises that seemed part of the life of the house itself; she imagined the very structure coming alive, communicating.

Now, she reminded herself of what Morris had told her. In these old houses there was even more wood and pipework, more of everything to expand and contract than there had been in that cottage. Or was the house trying to tell her something? Had it missed them, she wondered, as they left one by one, or was it glad?

She switched on the television set and turned the sound down completely and sat watching the images flit meaninglessly from one side of the bright screen to the other.

'The bathroom's through here,' Maggie said. 'Airing cupboard. There's a time switch for the water cylinder.'

'That's fine,' he said.

'The heating's separate. It's on a gas-boiler in the kitchen.' She showed him. 'I hope you'll be warm enough. I know Americans feel the cold over here.'

'Not this American. I don't like overheated buildings.'

They moved into the sitting-room. It faced north–east and they could see the lights of the tower blocks at Victoria.

'I like that,' he said. 'And all the chimney-pots. I like roofscapes.'

Alec had said the same when they first came to live in the house.

'They look better in daylight.'

They discussed the lease. Then he said, 'Why did you specify "visitors"? I mean, the real-estate office was definite about that.'

'It's our Rent Act,' she said. 'You can't get tenants out without a struggle if you want the flat back. So people like myself, who haven't got the time to fight court battles – or the inclination, for that matter – we ask agents to find us visiting professors, diplomats, the sort of people who are only going to stay for a limited time.'

He smiled. It was a large infectious smile that crinkled the corners of his eyes where there was a network of white lines in an otherwise sunburnt face. 'What if I like it over here?'

'Are you planning to immigrate to England? I thought it was usually the other way round.'

'I'm only kidding. I've come to see my father. He's ill. And I plan to take a real break. Haven't had a vacation for years. I'm going to buy myself a pedal cycle and drift through France until I find a place I like, and then sit in the sun and read.'

It was the sort of holiday she had always promised herself, but the opportunity had never arisen. First Alec had been too busy and then Alec had been dead.

'It sounds wonderful,' she said.

'It's something I've wanted to do since I was a kid. Maybe it's just nostalgia for lost youth. Maybe it would be more sensible to rent a car. But I kind of like the idea.'

'A car's *ordinary*.'

He nodded. 'That's true.'

'You'll find sheets and blankets in the cupboard in the bedroom. I don't think there's anything else.' She paused. 'I'm going to make myself some tea. Would you like a cup?'

'Thanks, but I'm bushed.'

'Then I'll leave you.' As she reached the door she indicated a telephone on the wall. 'That opens the front door. Just press down the bar and it opens automatically.'

'I don't think I'll be having visitors.'

'One thing: maybe I don't need to tell this to an American, but please make sure the front door is double-locked when you go out.'

'Don't worry. I'm careful.'

'Good night then.'

'Good night.'

She went down to her own flat feeling somewhat irritated with herself.

Ronnie Flower lay on the double bed watching Denise brush her hair. He loved watching her. She was naked except for an old silk kimono with wide sleeves. As she raised the brush he could see her right breast through the open sleeve. It was large and tempting, like Denise herself. She was a few years older than him, in her mid-thirties, and when they first started 'doing it', as he called it, he had said, 'I like a big woman. Something to get my hands on.'

'I'm not fruit and veg,' she had said. 'You keep that for the shop.'

'You know what I mean.'

'I know better than you.'

Now they were in her small flat a few streets away from the shop. Ronnie had always dreamed of a room like this. It was pink, and shiny with coloured lights. There were little glass animals on a side table which glittered and winked, and her nightdress was shoved into a cloth teddy-bear that smelled strongly of her scent.

She crossed one leg over another and the kimono fell away from her thigh. Ronnie said, 'Come back to bed.'

'I've just been there, thank you very much.'

'Come back again.'

'There's something the matter with you.'

'The matter?'

'You want to see a doctor, you do.'

'I can't help it. It's you.'

'Well, I been on my feet all day. I'm tired.' She worked in a hairdresser's salon in Camberwell, but lived north of the river because, as she said, there was a better class of person in Pimlico. There was an ex-husband somewhere in her background but she didn't talk about him much and Ronnie had the impression that he'd been inside.

'You won't be too tired when we go to Spain,' he said.

She brushed her hair with long angry sweeps. 'Oh, that.'

'Why do you say, "oh that"?'

'I get tired just thinking about it. You been talking about Spain ever since we been seeing each other.'

'It's going to happen. I got my eye on a place. Split level. With a swimming pool.'

'Oh yes.'

'And five acres. Near Malaga. And that's not far from Torremolinos.'

'When you've won the pools?'

'There're ways.'

'Ways! I'm telling you, I'm not going with your mother. It's either her or me.'

'Don't worry, I've got plans.'

'Plans! You?'

'You'll see. Come over here.'

'No. I told you.'

He slid off the bed, angry. 'D'you think I'm pretending? Listen. Things are happening. I reckon by the spring they'll have happened. You and me are going down to the Costa del Sol and we're gonna look around.'

'Oh yes?'

'Yes.' He suddenly grasped her fleshy upper arm. She tried to pull away but his grip was surprisingly strong.

'You're hurting.'

'You'll see,' he said. There was a note in his voice she had never heard before. She looked up into his face. She had never seen the expression in his eyes before either. His mouth was tight and his lips bloodless.

Her manner changed abruptly. 'All right love.' She got up and eased him gently towards the bed. 'I believe you.'

5

As Mr Hubert Ringham walked down Sutherland Street in Pimlico he looked as though he owned the place, and sometimes he felt he should. He had known so many people, both in his professional and private life, that his passage down the pavement was usually interrupted by little nods and becks and greetings, a wave, an inclination of the head, a faint smile. His was more a progress than a stroll and this was how he had planned it from the moment he had returned. Pretend that nothing had happened.

He was a student of human nature. He knew that to some people his act would always be an act but others, who perhaps had only heard rumours, would never be quite sure, and his presence – grand, patriarchal, almost aristocratic – would never allow them to be sure, would always throw them off balance. Gradually, even those who knew might begin to wonder. Mr Ringham had time. Time was not only a great healer, it was also a great obscurer. It blurred memory. Already he knew that his past had become blurred for many people. He was, in this respect only, a patient man.

Apart from the more degrading adjectives that had been applied to him when he'd had his little problem, the most usual was 'portly'. He was what might be described as an old-fashioned dresser. He was wearing a dark suit under a long black overcoat with frogging around the button-holes and an astrakhan collar, the kind affected by actor–managers in previous generations. On his head he wore a dark grey Homburg.

Mr Ringham gave the impression that these clothes were specially made for him by a dying generation of craftsmen perhaps now to be found only in Istanbul or Cairo. This was not true. He had also been described as a fine figure of a man, and this *was* true.

Now, with the curve of his stomach thrust out before him, his arms hanging almost motionless by his sides, his palms facing backwards, he walked towards Sebastopol Square. He should have been enjoying the winter sunshine. Instead, behind his benign carapace he felt the same old rising tide of anger and envy. The square did not look sleazy and decayed to Mr Ringham. It was a place of beauty, one to be desired. He should have had it by now, the whole thing. Then there would have been no stopping him. He raised a hand in greeting to Ronnie Flower, who was talking to a boy with a shaven head. He had known Ronnie since he was a child; a fat, nasty little boy coming from a rotten family.

'Lovely day,' Mr Ringham said.

'Yeah. How's it going?'

Mr Ringham did not reply. It was not a question. Nor would he have replied had it been. The boy turned and glanced at him and he was chilled by the cold grey eyes. Scum, he thought, and passed by. He felt a sudden flare of anger mushroom in him so fast that he had to swallow quickly or he might have choked. This was the only thing wrong with the Crimea; scum like this. He had a moment of ecstasy as he held the boy down and beat him to death with a hammer, then the boy turned away and Mr Ringham entered Sebastopol Square.

He looked at the Square with the eye of lust. Many years ago, more than he cared to contemplate, he had entered the world in a room under the eaves of Number Twelve, where his mother had worked first as a parlourmaid and then as a cook-general. As a child he had played in the gardens. In those days there had been well tended lawns and shrubberies and a red clay tennis court. There had been a proper gardener to look after it, who had marked its lines every Friday afternoon, all fresh and white for the weekend. He remembered men in cream flannels and girls in white dresses, sitting on the verandah of the tennis hut. He paused, looking at Numbers Twelve and Fourteen, at the corrugated-iron over the windows, the ruined garden, the abandoned cars. The war had started the decay; all those foreigners. It had been continued by the bomb which had obliterated Numbers Thirty-three to Thirty-seven, where they backed onto the railway tracks. They had been rebuilt as modern houses of porridge-coloured bricks, which was not to Mr Ringham's taste, though he knew they were both expensive and luxurious inside. He preferred the old style, with porticos and pillars and mouldings. Further on down the Square, Number Twenty-one was being done up, so were Number Nineteen, Number Two and Number Eight.

Twelve and Fourteen would soon be the only houses left in their post-war dilapidation. God, what he couldn't do with them! A hotel, perhaps, flats, houses like they used to be, full of grace and sophistication. He saw himself in one of them. 'Hubert Ringham, Esq, of Sebastopol Square.' Instead, they belonged to some faceless company, probably incorporated in Jersey for tax reasons. That was the trouble with London these days, it was owned by absentee landlords: Americans, Arabs, Nigerians. Things had changed. 'Faceless' was the word. His only contact with the owners had been a letter asking him to collect the rents and send the cheque – such as it was, he thought – to a London address once a month.

He crossed the street, picking his way between the

rubbish and the parked cars, and paused outside Number Twelve. This was where they had found old Nedza. Slipped and banged his head. Well, what can you expect at that age if you go out on freezing winter days?

He began to descend the basement steps. He'd better be careful himself. If he fell, his weight might finish him.

Sophie Mendel heard the footsteps and for a moment she thought it was Stefan. She had been changing the budgerigar's water and now she closed the cage and stood waiting for his double knock. Then she remembered: it couldn't be Stefan. But it could be Dr Hollis. She had promised to take Sophie to see Stefan, but she had said three o'clock and it was only lunchtime. Had she had her lunch? Was that past?

She looked at the cheap alarm-clock on the mantelpiece, next to the three photographs. No, it wasn't three yet.

The knock came, loud and frightening. She remained where she was, holding her breath, listening. No one could see in. No one knew she was there, or at least, they could not be certain.

'Mrs Mendel!' She knew that booming voice. 'Mrs Mendel! It's Mr Ringham. Mr Hubert Ringham.'

She opened the door, unlocking locks and sliding back bolts and taking off the chain so that it was like opening the gate in the bailey of some besieged castle.

'Good morning, Mrs Mendel! And how are you today?' Mr Ringham filled the doorway as he entered.

'I forgot,' she said.

'First Thursday. Always the first Thursday.'

'Ja. A person can forget. But I don't forget the money.'

'That's good. You have it then?'

'*Naturlich.*'

She went to the top drawer of an old mahogany chest and came back with a large brown envelope which had seen much use and which was folded at the top, closed with a small bulldog clip. She pressed the clip to open but it slipped away from her. She tried again. The clip seemed stiffer than usual.

'May I ?' said Mr Ringham in a voice that Othello might have envied.

'No. I do it.' She managed to open it, took out a small pile of money.

In turn, Mr Ringham reached into the capacious inside pocket of his overcoat and brought out a large leather wallet of the sort German and Austrian waiters use. He took the money, placed it in the wallet, then took the book which Sophie was proffering. He entered the amount, the date, then initialled the entry.

'All paid up for another month,' he said.

There was a slightly bitter edge to his voice. This was the room where his mother had worked all those years before.

'Count it,' Mrs Mendel said.

'I already have.' A pittance, he thought. She paid a pittance. Controlled tenant. He put the rent money away in the deep inner pocket and looked around the room, seeing the damp patches on the wallpaper, the scarring on the doors. Original doors, he thought. Must be. He might have touched those very handles as a child. You went through into the kitchen and there was a door that looked like a cupboard that led to a staircase. When he was six or seven he thought of it as his secret staircase. He remembered his mother carrying the dishes upstairs. When he was older he would help her, bringing a couple of plates or a toast-rack. He remembered her lisle stockings on the stairs in front of him, and trying to look up her skirt. The light was too dim to see much.

'How's Mr Nedza?' he asked, more to fill in time while his mind probed at an idea.

'You been to see him?' she asked.

41

'Hospitals!' He waved a large white hand. 'But I will.'

'Save yourself. He don't recognise even me.'

'It comes from living here,' Mr Ringham said. 'Death-traps, these old houses. It's lucky in a way he fell where he did.'

'Breaking your head is lucky?'

'You mistake my meaning. Think if it had happened to him upstairs. No one might have found him for days. That's what can happen, Mrs Mendel.'

She looked at him, seeing Berlin before the war. She had worked as a waitress then in a *Konditorei* on the Ku-dam. Sometimes when business was slack she would stand near the door and watch the people as they passed by. This was how they had looked: long dark overcoats, astrakhan collars, Homburgs. Leo had had a hat like this. He had been very proud of it. How many times had he worn it? Three, four? She remembered they had gone to the Tiergarten and strolled up to the Brandenburg Gate. That was the last summer before the war: he had been wearing it then. She had looked after it for him, putting it with her own hats in a box, but after 1944 she had never seen it again. It had disappeared into the past, like Leo.

'We're none of us getting any younger, Mrs Mendel,' Mr Ringham was saying. 'I don't want to alarm you, but it's only commonsense. Who would know?'

'What?'

'Well, an accident. You're getting out of your bath. You slip. They don't find you for forty-eight hours. You should think about it.'

She thought about it often, but she wasn't going to think about it for Mr Ringham.

'It's called sheltered accommodation,' he said. 'The council could get you something. Nurses on call. Buttons you push. Special phones. They have these computers now. You push a button, you talk to a man on the switchboard. Two minutes later there's someone to help you. I mean, it's only commonsense.'

'The council already asked me,' Mrs Mendel said coldly.

'And your property company.'

'It's not *mine*.'

'They wrote a letter to me and to Mr Nedza and Miss Krause. Three, four times they write. Then they send that estate agent, that Mr Deacon. We say same to everybody. This is where we live; you will *not* put us out!'

'Nobody wants you out, Mrs Mendel. I wouldn't put it like . . .'

'Yes, they do. Pimlico House. Fifth floor. That's where they want me. Well, I say no. This is my home. What I want is to be left alone.'

He rose ponderously. 'You should think about it. You're alone now . . .' He paused after the word, giving it extra meaning. 'Miss Oppenheimer's gone. Miss Krause has gone. Mr Nedza's never coming back, believe me.' He opened the door. 'It's for your own good, Mrs Mendel.'

He left behind him a faint smell, perhaps impregnated into his coat, which she recognised. Turnips. The smell brought back Germany just after the war. She had been in the north for a short while looking for work, for food, anything to keep Leni and herself alive. What she'd found was turnips, the sort farmers had once strewn on the fields to feed the stock. After the war, human beings fought over them. Leni's face was clear in her mind, the Leni who was a few years older than the photograph. She tried not to think about her, instead concentrating on what she would wear that afternoon, not that there was much choice.

'My dark brown coat,' she said to Winston. 'And my hat with the grapes.' The budgie hopped up onto its swing. 'He likes the one with the grapes.'

43

Stefan had said the plastic grapes were so lifelike he wanted to eat them. He said they were Muscat. Maybe he was right, she didn't know one grape from another. 'I wear it just in case he wakes up,' she told the bird.

Stefan Nedza seemed slightly better, Maggie thought, as she and Sophie looked down at the figure on the bed. The tube was still in his nose but they had taken some of the bandages off his head. He was relaxed, and the lines on his face had smoothed out and he looked younger than he was. His eyes were closed, his breathing shallow. She felt a sense of despair. What could they, the doctors, the medical profession as a whole, what could they do for this old man now?

'He looks better.' Sophie was sitting on the far side of the bed. The grey light from the high window of the room fell on the bunch of plastic grapes on her hat.

'I spoke to the consultant,' Maggie said. 'There's no change, I'm afraid.'

Sophie shifted her handbag on her lap. 'You in a hurry? We should go?'

'I didn't mean that. I've got time. Let's just sit. Who knows?'

'A miracle?' Sophie said.

'Not quite that. It sometimes happens that they suddenly regain consciousness. We don't know exactly why.'

They were silent for a moment and Maggie watched Sophie under her eyelids. She wasn't looking too good. She seemed thinner than when she had last been examined in the surgery. That was the trouble with so many old people, they stopped eating. Her brown coat was becoming threadbare. And the hat. God, the hat. It was like something from a movie of the forties. Women having tea in an Odeon. But under the hat was the face of a woman who had lived a great deal, who had seen a lot; the eyes bright, birdlike.

'I like your hat,' Maggie said. 'I don't think I've seen it before.'

'He liked the grapes. Muscat. That's what he said.' Sophie paused. 'A bit strange, ain't it? All the way from Cracow to die here in Pimlico.'

'Don't give up hope.'

'Hope? I hope he never wakes. Better for him to slip away.'

That was true, Maggie thought, but doctors weren't supposed to react like that. 'Have you known him long?' she said, to make conversation. She was surprised at the answer.

'I know Stefan forty years. From nineteen forty-six. When the houses were still the club.'

'Which houses?'

'Twelve and Fourteen.'

'I didn't know they were a club.'

'Before you were born, *ja*? The Red Cross Pop-in Club. For foreigners who couldn't speak English too well. They had classes and picture shows. There was a library and a tea-room and a bar for the evening. When I first came to England with Morris he said, You must learn English proper. So I went there. And I met Miss Oppenheimer and Miss Krause. All the others.'

'And Stefan?'

'Ah, he came to pick up girls. I think after his first marriage, maybe. Very handsome. He was a gunner. They say he shot down four German planes by himself.'

'In the Polish Air Force?'

'No, no. Here. The Poles come here. They escape. They form a special squadron with the RAF.'

'So you knew each other in those days?'

'That's right. Then I didn't come to the club, not regularly. But after Morris died it was place to go, some

45

place to see people I knew. A person can be lonely when the husband dies.'

'I know,' Maggie said.

'Then it changed from a club. There was so few left, how can you run a club? So they turned it into flats and they rented to us.'

'The Red Cross?'

'At first the Red Cross. But then they sold the houses. Two, three times they been sold. Property companies. Stefan came back after the third Mrs Nedza died. He went off to live with another lady after a while and when she died he came back for good.'

Maggie had a sad impression of all these old lonely folk coming back like homing pigeons to Sebastopol Square. It was as though Sophie read her mind, for she said, 'When people get old they want to go back where they were born. Life makes a circle. But Stefan couldn't go back to Poland; to me, Berlin was finished. Maria Krause came from Leipzig, Lily from the Sudetenland. Sebastopol Square was where we had once all been young. That's why we came back.'

They talked on for fifteen or twenty minutes, Maggie mostly listening, identifying. She herself had grown up in Pimlico, born in one of the big houses in Warwick Square, living a life so different from the life of Sebastopol Square, and yet only a few streets away. When she had been ten or eleven the Crimea was a place to avoid; she had been warned about it by her parents, and she had avoided it. But Alec had not thought like that. 'It's where we're needed most,' he'd said. To her the Crimea was still a strange land.

Stefan did not move the entire time and when a nurse came to shift him into a different position they left. They went down the long corridor towards the entrance. The afternoon visitors were arriving. She helped Sophie into the small Renault in one of the private spaces outside the main door and was about to back out when a taxi drew up at the steps. Something about the figure who got out caused her to pause for a moment. She couldn't see him plainly, then he straightened up from paying the driver and moved lightly up the steps.

Sophie said, 'Such a big man.'

'Yes,' Maggie said. It was her lodger, Bill Seago.

6

It had been freezing since Maggie had returned from the hospital. Now it was 6.30 and surgery was over. You could always tell when the weather was severe: the old didn't come out. She made her way up to her flat on the first floor with a sense of relief, but also partly retaining the depression which had settled on her as she had sat at the old man's bedside. She had driven Sophie home and something had occurred which had left a bad taste in her mouth. Sophie had wanted to be dropped outside Flower's shop. Maggie had said, 'You know, Mrs Mendel, I'm sure Ronnie Flower would deliver for you. Or if you'd let me know what you want, I'd pick up whatever you need on my rounds. It'd be no trouble.'

'No,' Sophie had said. It wasn't a no that said, thanks very much, it was a flat refusal. Maggie had been somewhat taken aback at its vehemence.

'I only meant it as a way of helping you, keeping you indoors in the cold weather.'

'I been shopping all my life,' Sophie said. 'They ain't going to stop me.'

'They?'

'They! Muggers!'

She had heard Sophie on muggers before. She might be right, for all that Maggie knew. All the more reason, she thought, to keep Sophie off the streets on these dingy afternoons. In summer it wasn't so bad, there were many more people about, but now Sebastopol Square was like a no-man's-land entered only by a few.

She had said, 'Mrs Mendel, there's something I've been meaning to mention to you.'

'Oh?' Immediately suspicious.

'Have you ever thought of giving up your flat?'

'What?'

'I could get you into . . .'

'Pimlico House?'

'I wasn't going to suggest that. There's a new complex of old people's flats being put up near the river. Studio flats, with buzzers linked to a central computer and a nurse on . . .'

Sophie was fumbling at the seat-belt, unlocking it.

'Mrs Mendel?'

The old woman had the door open and was getting out into the street. She peered into the car. 'I come to you for advice about my health. My life I can run.' She turned away, leaving the door open.

Maggie had watched her, surprised and hurt. What can you do, she had thought as she slammed the door and started the engine. You try to help and it gets thrown in your face. Still, you had to admire her spirit.

Now, as she changed out of her day clothes and stood in her bra and pants in front of the long mirror in her bedroom, she took a careful look at herself. She saw a woman of medium height, full-breasted and wide-hipped, a face with high cheek-bones and wide-spaced brown eyes. Her brown hair was cut short. She wasn't entirely unpleased with this view of herself. She had put on a bit of weight in the last year and was looking better than the concentration camp victim she'd become after Alec's death. Now she could contemplate putting on a bikini with only partial apprehension.

But then the last vestiges of her depression blurred her view of herself and she thought, One day you'll be like

49

Sophie Mendel. And she thought, What a bloody waste.

She put on a long green and gold caftan and went into the sitting-room. She could hear Bill Seago moving about in the flat above.

She'd had only women lodgers until now. There had been an American philosophy major who had come to do a PhD at London University, and an elderly writer from New Zealand who had spent her time at the British Library. They'd had a perfectly amicable working arrangement and she had been neither glad nor sorry when they left. But now things were different. She was uneasy at the thought of a man upstairs and yet, conversely, glad. She thought of the figure going up the hospital steps, so big and yet so light on his feet. It gave her a feeling of reassurance to have him there.

The telephone rang. She picked it up and a voice said, 'Hello, Margaret.'

'Who's that?'

'Kenneth.'

'Who?'

'Kenneth!'

'God, I'm sorry! I was miles away. And I think there's something the matter with the line. I didn't recognise your voice.'

'That's all right.' There was a touch of irritation in his tone. 'I'll be a few minutes late.' She suddenly remembered that it was Thursday. 'There's a new Thai restaurant in Kensington. How does that grab you?'

'Kenneth, I'm going to have to call off tonight. I think I may be getting 'flu.'

'Oh.' There was a pause. 'Have you got something to take?'

'Yes, Kenneth. I'm a doctor.'

He laughed drily. 'I suppose it'll have to be next week then. I might be able to get away on Sunday.'

'I'm on duty on Sunday.' That was a lie.

'Next Thursday, then.'

'Yes. Next Thursday. I'm sorry, Kenneth.'

'Look after yourself. 'Bye.'

She put the telephone down with a slight sense of guilt. She heard the pipes gurgling upstairs and knew Seago was having a shower. She wondered about him. She had not known many Americans and the one or two she had met in recent years professionally and socially had all been from the Middle West. The men had worn plaid trousers and their wives had wanted to talk about shopping in Harrods. She found she hadn't much in common with them. Seago seemed different. She stood at the window for some time, looking at the cold night, thinking about him. He must have been at the hospital to see his father. She wondered if he was terminally ill. That would explain why his son had taken the flat for three months.

There was a knock on her flat door. When she opened it, Seago was standing outside. He was dressed in dark grey hopsack trousers, black loafers and a white polo-neck sweater. She could smell his fresh soapy showery smell.

'Sorry to bother you,' he said, 'but the phone upstairs seems to be dead.'

'It's a new one,' she said. 'I don't think it's settled down yet. If you want to make a call, use mine. I'll have yours seen to in the morning.'

She showed him the telephone in the hall and went into her sitting-room, closing the door. She heard the low rumble of his voice and then he tapped lightly on the sitting-room door, opened it and said, 'Thanks.'

'Apart from the phone, is everything else all right?'

'Just fine.'

There was a pause, then she said, 'I was about to have a drink. Would you like to join me?'

'That's the best offer I've had all day.' He smiled, and the large, boyish face broke open like a melon. 'I was about to have one myself.' He closed the door behind

51

him. Immediately the room seemed smaller, but more cheerful and more interesting.

'What can I get you?'

'Scotch.'

'Lots of ice?'

'Just one piece, or none, if it's any trouble. I'm trying not to be a cliché American.'

She smiled. 'I can see that.'

They talked generalities for a while: weather, traffic, plays and movies. She gave him another drink. He was sitting on the sofa, leaning back, his arm along the top, hand hanging limply. He looked completely relaxed.

He told her he came from Boston. 'Ever been there?'

'About three years ago, with my husband. We stayed at the Sheraton and then drove into the country. It was November and we'd missed the best of the Fall, but it was lovely, anyway.'

'You were there with your husband?'

'He died nearly two years ago.'

'I'm sorry.'

She wanted to keep off the subjects of death and widowhood, and poured herself another glass of wine.

Before he could ask any more questions she said quickly, 'What do you do?'

'Build roads. Dams. Or at least I did. I was with the United Nations. Worked mostly in the Third World.' He finished his drink and rose. 'Thank you. That was nice.'

As she saw him to the door she said, 'How is your father?'

'I just called the hospital.' He indicated her telephone. 'No change.'

She frowned, puzzled. 'You didn't see him then?'

He shook his head. 'I rubber-necked around London. Westminster Abbey. The Tate. The National Gallery.'

'But I thought . . .'

He waited politely for her to finish.

52

'Nothing,' she said. 'It doesn't matter.'

Sophie listened to the house. She was in her little sitting-room with the television switched on, the sound down. It was there for companionship, as was Winston. Half the time she did not even look at it but sat with her head cocked, listening to the old timbers move. What was it trying to tell her? To get out? To go into one of those flats for old people? To give away her belongings (who would buy them now?) and move into Pimlico House and become a vegetable like Lily Oppenheimer on the fifth floor, turning the pages of her bank book, unable even to count?

An image on the screen caught her eye. She saw a street filled with rubble. A man running. The snout of a large gun came slowly round the corner of a building, enlarging to become a tank. Berlin? Budapest? Prague? More likely Berlin, with all the rubble and shattered buildings. They must be showing some old news-reels, telling again the story that she knew so well.

The images made her think again of Leni. They had come back from the north, for you couldn't live on turnips. Their 'house' was only a cellar with a heap of bricks and broken masonry above it. No water. No sanitation. No electricity. They had lived there that first winter after the war. She had found work – she was one of the lucky ones – in a canteen that served British other ranks. That was where she'd met Morris. Morris Mendel, journeyman printer. Corporal Morris Mendel of the Royal Hampshire Fusiliers, part of the conquering army. He gave her chocolate and nylons and she gave him what he wanted. Then she swapped the nylons and chocolate for bread and powdered egg, a little bit of meat, some fish, a banana, whatever was available on the black market, and fuel, of course, and kept Leni and herself alive.

Leni was thirteen and a half then and she was going to a little school in the next block. Also in a cellar. It was extraordinary how they had managed to get things started again in a ruined city.

Sophie had liked to get home in daylight. The streets were not safe. There were Russian troops and American, British and French, all on the lookout. And if it wasn't soldiers, it was the street gangs; fourteen year olds with eyes like old men and ribs sticking out. They called themselves names from the war, the Panzers, the SS, the Wolves. One afternoon she had come home later than usual and found two of them with Leni. One was holding her down, the other was on top of her. Sophie had never been able to recall clearly what happened in the next few seconds. The knife must have been on the table. Leni had been preparing vegetable soup. When Sophie's mind cleared there was blood spraying from the boy's neck and the other boy had fled. She remembered the blood, it came up like a red speckled fan. She was trying to cut his throat but he pushed her away and staggered up the steps into the street and she never saw either of them again, though she heard on the grapevine that one had died.

Leni never recovered. In the spring she developed pleurisy, then pneumonia. By the time Morris managed to get some penicillin it was too late.

In the summer Morris was being sent back to England to be demobilised. He asked her to come with him, to marry him, to live in England. She had already lost Leo, her first husband, somewhere on the Russian front, and then Leni. What was there to stay in Berlin for?

But now, she had lost her strength and agility and whatever power she'd had in that cellar . . . that was gone, and she seemed to be back where she had started. Sebastopol Square was not rubble, no tank was entering from Inkerman Street, but the pavements smelled of danger, just like those in Berlin so many years ago. Except now there was no Leo, no Morris and no Leni. They were simply three photographs without life. And now she needed them more than she had ever needed them, for she was sure that someone was trying to kill her.

After she got out of Dr Hollis's car she had walked home with her few purchases in her string bag. They had been standing by the broken gate of the gardens. The heads reminded her of prisoners she had seen one day during the war, being marched up the Budapesterstrasse. Russian prisoners, they said, being taken to a camp in Saxony. She thought she heard a laugh, then someone shouted. She couldn't make out what he said. She hurried, reaching at the same time for her key so that she would not lose a moment. It was the key that saved her. It dropped from her cold fingers onto the steps leading down to the basement. She had already begun to descend. She stopped. The key lay on the step below her. She was about to step down to retrieve it when she saw that it lay on a sheet of milky ice. The ice covered the central area of the step and the one below it. She descended carefully on the side of the steps, retrieved the key and, holding onto the railing, let herself down to her flat. She opened the door and flung it closed behind her, rattling the bolts and turning the locks and putting up the chain. She stood there for a long moment in sudden terror, wondering whether anyone might be there, waiting for her, but all she heard was the croaking of the budgie.

'If I say anything they will say Sophie Mendel is getting senile,' she said to Winston. 'Sophie Mendel must go to Pimlico House.' But she wasn't senile. 'Otherwise, tell me, if a bottle smashes, where was the glass?'

Another thought came: she had never taken a milk delivery. Nor had anyone else in the house.

7

'Like a fist,' Mrs Flower said. 'Just like fingers gripping and twisting.'

Her bedroom smelled of a mixture of old food and medicines. Maggie could separate Vick and some sort of camphorated oil. The air was stale and overheated and she doubted that the window had been opened in years.

'And of course I been running all night.'

Ronnie hovered in the doorway, blocking it with his plump soft body.

'Up and down the stairs,' Mrs Flower said.

'And if she fell, I wouldn't be able to pick her up,' Ronnie said.

'What did you have for supper?' Maggie said to the mountain of blankets which fortunately hid most of Mrs Flower.

'A pork pie.' She winced at the memory.

Maggie had known for years what people said about the Flowers, how they hated to throw anything away. 'Did you look at the sell-by date?'

'You don't think . . .!' Mrs Flower began. 'We wouldn't keep no out-of-date stuff.'

'How would *you* know?' Ronnie said crossly.

'Pork pies can be dangerous.'

'I told her the date,' Ronnie said. 'I had liver and bacon.'

'And how have you been?'

'Never felt a thing.'

'And you went out and left me!' Mrs Flower said.

'That was *before* you was ill,' Ronnie said. 'Saturday night. You got to go out of a Saturday night.'

'Anyway, the pain's gone now, has it, Mrs Flower?'

'Only just. But I'm still running.'

The picture of this mountainous woman in swift motion was instantly suppressed by Maggie.

'I'll give you a prescription for kaolin and morphine. Your son can have it filled at the chemist on Victoria Station. They're open on a Sunday, I think.'

She went down the staircase, which was lined with boxes of tinned fruit and corned beef. And then across a landing stacked high with model aircraft kits and down through the shop and outside.

In spite of the fact that it was London, the air smelled fresh by comparison with the Flowers' house. The weather had been brilliantly clear in the past twenty-four hours; sunny all day with a freezing easterly airstream coming in from Russia. All the smog seemed to have blown away, but the nights were well below freezing.

She walked to her car and saw in Sebastopol Square a large figure standing near Sophie Mendel's house. For a second she thought it was Mr Ringham, but he didn't collect rents on a Sunday morning. In the same instant the figure turned and she saw it was Bill Seago. They were less than fifty yards apart and he raised his hand in greeting and came towards her.

'I've been having a look round,' he said.

'There's not much to see in Pimlico.'

'I guess it's more for exercise than anything else. I feel restless on days like this. Don't like to be cooped up.'

'My husband felt the same. We used to go into the country. Alec would find bridle paths and we'd walk for hours.'

'Are you on duty?'

'No. This was a private patient. One of the few I have.'

'Feel like a walk?'

'Where to?'

'You lead,' he said.

They walked to the Thames, across Chelsea Bridge and along the River Walk in Battersea Park. They didn't talk much. She was of medium height but felt small next to him.

'How is your father?' she said.

'Not too good.'

They were walking quickly and she felt her cheeks stinging in the breeze.

'This is Boston weather,' he said.

There were streaks of mist on the river that the sun was burning away. 'Look!' She pointed across to the far bank and a block of red-brick apartments half hidden by mist. It was a strange, almost medieval sight. They looked at it for several minutes before going on.

On the way back he took her arm as they crossed the Queenstown Road. It was the sort of thing Alec had done. Seago kept his hand under her elbow once they had reached the far pavement.

Her feelings about him were complicated. She enjoyed his company, but why had he lied? She had *seen* him going up the hospital steps.

Then another thought came to her. Perhaps his father wasn't there at all. Perhaps he'd gone to the hospital for some other reason. There could be a dozen different ones. He didn't look like a man who lied. His face was too open, too frank. She decided to forget it – and from that moment she started to enjoy herself.

They walked along the Embankment and crossed into the maze of streets that made up the heart of Pimlico. And, suddenly, Kenneth was facing her. He had come round a corner, with a young girl by his side. She smiled and greeted him. He swung his eyes away from her, pretending he had not seen her. His face wore a bitter angry expression.

'Wasn't that . . .?' Bill began.

'The estate agent.'

He seemed to wait for her to continue, but she kept silent. After a moment he said, 'It's nearly lunchtime. I'm hungry. How about you?'

They went to a restaurant in the King's Road.

After they had ordered he said, 'Tell me about your husband. Alec, was it?'

She didn't answer for a moment, knowing he was waiting.

'Don't you like to talk about it?'

'Not much.'

'When you mention him, you make it sound as though he's just away on holiday.'

Sometimes that was the way she felt. As though the door was going to open any minute and he was going to walk in.

'He died in a climbing accident in the Cairngorms in Scotland.'

'Where were you?'

'Here.'

'Have some more.' He indicated a dish of French fries.

She shook her head. She was remembering the telephone call. Suddenly, she began to talk.

The call had come from a policeman in Aviemore. The rich, Highland voice, telling her that her husband had fallen and that they were bringing him down. And, yes, he was alive. A few broken bones, but she'd better get up there. And she'd said he was climbing with a friend and the policeman had said he was afraid the other climber was dead. She had thought, Poor Hamish. He and Alec had climbed together ever since the three of them had been at university: Scotland, Austria, Switzerland. The call had come about half-past five in the afternoon of a dark wet spring day and she had driven all night, thanking fate it was Hamish, not Alec, and then feeling guilty. She reached Aviemore in the grey drizzly dawn.

At the police station they told her that the Mountain Rescue Team had brought the two climbers off the top about midnight. Alec was in a private room at the local hospital. She went there immediately and a staff nurse had taken her to the room. There was a figure on the bed, arm in cast, blankets up to his mouth.

'That's not Alec,' she had whispered.

The nurse had looked at the label tied to the end of the bed. 'Not Dr Hollis?'

'No.'

Then she had to identify him. His nose and the left side of his face, including his eye, had gone, disappeared. It was a sight she would never forget. It was something she had tried to overlay, bury, cover up, expunge from her mind – and now Seago had forced it to the surface again and for a moment she hated him.

'Now it's my turn,' she said. 'What about your wife?'

'I don't have one.'

'Dead? Divorced? Separated?'

He was silent, and suddenly she felt drained. 'I'm sorry. It's just that I haven't talked about Alec for a long time.'

'Why not?'

Kenneth had mainly wanted to explore his own widower-hood. Anyhow, he wasn't really the person she wanted to communicate with. 'No one to talk to, I suppose.'

They drank the last of the wine and he asked for the bill.

'Well?' she said.

'I'm divorced. It's not an unusual story, I guess. My work meant a lot of bachelor living in the backblocks of the world. Stella didn't like being alone. It's as simple as that.'

He smiled and said, 'Now it's my turn to say, well?'

60

'Well what?'

'Confession's supposed to be cathartic, isn't it? Are you feeling better?'

'Physician, heal thyself?'

'Something like that. Do you like being a doctor?'

'Yes. And you, do you like being an engineer?'

'When I'm out there in the desert, or wherever, I long for this. And when I'm here I feel trapped. Makes for schizophrenia.'

They went out into the freezing afternoon.

The alarm-clock woke Mr Hubert Ringham at 8 a.m. He opened one eye, then the other, and raised his head gingerly from the pillow, testing the first throb that would indicate how far he had overdone it the night before. It wasn't too bad, not when you considered its foundations. It had started with Guinness and champagne. Black velvet. You couldn't beat it. Black velvet and oysters were always supposed to be the recipe. But oysters were messy. You had to open them. Anyway, Denise had said to him, 'You don't need oysters. That's the last thing you need. If you was to eat a couple of dozen oysters of a Sunday night, no one would be safe.'

Denise. She was really some woman. What a difference she'd made to his life. Seeing her was something to look forward to all week. A box of cooked prawns, a bottle of champagne, couple of pints of Guinness. And that was just for starters. Then to the West End for dinner. None of your Soho muck, but a decent hotel where you could go to the carvery and eat as much roast beef as you liked. Mr Ringham was very fond of roast beef. So was Denise. That's what he liked about her. She wasn't trying to slim all the time. She could match him glass for glass, slice for slice, Yorkshire for Yorkshire, spud for spud – and then Black Forest gateau. And, of course, more wine. And then back to her place, he with a bottle of brandy in his hand.

All that pink lighting and the shiny underwear and under the underwear Denise, all pink flesh.

Flesh was a word Mr Ringham particularly liked. Just hearing it or seeing it written down stimulated various glands in his body. He had once told this to Denise and she had laughed and said, 'You sound like a cannibal, you do.'

Thinking about her produced in him a desire for her company, but she'd already be on her way south of the river to the hairdresser's shop. He'd have to get moving, too. Ten-past eight. Monday morning. Winter. Much nicer to have Denise cuddling up in bed to him right now and not having to get up and go tramping round the freezing streets, knocking on doors, asking for a few pounds here and a few pounds there. Not very dignified for someone of Mr Ringham's substance.

What he wanted was a quick killing. In, out. Money in the bank. He might even ask Denise to marry him. But you had to have something to offer. Why marry him otherwise? No, give her security and all the rest would follow.

He got out of bed and drew the curtains, letting in the grey morning light. It was a small bedroom, typical of an Inkerman Street house that had not been done up; worn brown haircord on the floor, blocked-up fireplace, damp patches on the wallpaper. He couldn't bring someone like Denise to live here.

He looked across the street to Sebastopol Square and saw Ronnie Flower begin to put out the vegetable boxes and the odds and ends under the awning. He'd be worth a few bob, Mr Ringham thought; he and that fat cow of a mother of his. Though they said she held the purse-strings.

But the shop and the house must be worth something even if you just pulled it down and started again. Mightn't even have to do that. Most of the old corner shops were restaurants now with fancy Spanish or Greek names, or betting shops, or take-aways. Next to Numbers Twelve and Fourteen, too.

Property, he thought, going into the cold linoleum-floored bathroom and starting to shave. Property. His eyes were yellow, his skin much the same.

A property developer. That was something of substance. Borrow the money, buy, sell, profit in the bank. But who was going to lend Mr Ringham money? Not the banks nor the building societies. Collateral. That's what they wanted and even if he'd had the collateral there was always the little problem he'd had in the past.

He lathered his face and began to scrape at it with his razor. He'd have to find someone with the money. A partnership. *You* put up the money, *I* find the property. That sort of deal. But who had money like that? There was Charles Fabel, Charlie 'The Nob' Fabel, who'd been in the next cell to him in the Scrubs. But Charlie would never come up with money. And if he did, he'd want guarantees, and Mr Ringham knew the kind of people Charlie hired to enforce the guarantees. No, not Charlie. His mind went through a list of names, but some were dead and some were broke and others had got lost over the years. He suddenly realised that he knew no one of substance except . . . well, except Kenneth Deacon. And the more he thought of him, the more possible it seemed.

He finished shaving and patted his cheeks till the blood flowed. 'You're not just a pretty face,' he said to his reflection in the mirror.

8

The crematorium was in Camden Town and Maggie
got stuck well short of that in a traffic jam in the Euston
Road. By the time she had extricated herself and was
wriggling through the back streets it was already past
half-past eleven, when the service was scheduled to start.
The crematorium was a small building with an exhausted
strip of grass in front and some potted shrubs to give it a
'Garden of Remembrance' look. She double-parked, went
up the steps and opened one of the big double doors.

She slipped into the back pew and an undertakers'
assistant handed her a hymn book. The place was like a
small church and dimly lit. The coffin stood on a table
on a platform. It was surrounded by flowers. At one side
was an electronic organ. A man was playing a Bach chor-
ale and a priest was in attendance, wearing cassock and
surplice.

A few rows ahead of her stood the large figure of
Mr Ringham in his long black overcoat, and next to
him the diminutive shape of Sophie Mendel wearing
her black straw hat with the grapes. She must have come
with Ringham, Maggie thought, for she had telephoned
to offer a lift and received a brusque refusal.

Then she saw, beyond Mr Ringham's portly figure,
someone else in the front pew where the family mourners normally stood. Even in the half-light, there was no
mistaking the big shoulders and sandy hair of Bill Seago.

For a moment she thought she must have come to the wrong service. But it couldn't be: this was the time and this was the place.

At that moment a pair of curtains slowly began to close, hiding the coffin. The organ swelled. The priest said a prayer and mourners were filing out into the cold air of North London. She watched Sophie Mendel and Mr Ringham climb into a taxi and drive off. She waited. After a moment the doors opened again and Bill Seago came out with the priest. They shook hands, then Seago came down the steps towards her. He saw her, stopped, came on again.

'I waited to see if you wanted a lift,' she said.

He nodded slowly, but the way he looked at her she knew he was not only accepting her offer but putting together a series of thoughts. 'I need a drink more than a lift,' he said.

'There's a pub along the road.'

They went to The Dog and Fox and entered the 'snug'. It was empty and smelled strongly of last night's beer and stale cigarette smoke.

He fetched them each a whisky and they sat down at a table. She said, 'When I saw you I thought I was at the wrong service. But I wasn't, was I?'

'When I first saw you I thought you were, too.'

'I was at Stefan Nedza's funeral. Whose were you at?'

'My father's.'

He saw the astonishment on her face and said, 'It sounds complicated, but it isn't. He was a Pole who fought for the RAF during the war and married an English girl. My mother died when I was two and he couldn't look after me. Or didn't want to. Not at that stage, anyway. I guess it was difficult for him: no money, no job. Anyway, he sent me to my mother's sister. She'd been a GI bride and had gone to live in Boston. My uncle was a garage mechanic, then owned his own garage. He was doing okay. They could afford to keep me.

'I was always scheduled to come back. That's what he said. When the time was right. But the right time never came. He married again and they still didn't have much money. So what had started off as a temporary expedient became permanent. I was adopted and took my uncle's name, went to high school, then MIT.

'I kept in touch with my father, or at least he kept in touch with me, once a year at Christmas. The second marriage didn't last, but there always seemed to be some woman to look after him. Real ladies' man. I used to enjoy his letters. They were full of wild spelling and wilder grammar, but they were fun, full of life. He did some selling and clerking, but you could see he was never going to be a success at anything. He always had plans, though. Sort of a Micawber figure. Success was just around the corner; good times were over the next hill.

'I guess he did find someone permanent near the end, someone who was as fond of him as he was of her. Probably he'd run out of sexual steam by that time and settled down. Let me get you another?'

'No, I have patients to see. You have one.'

He fetched another drink and lit a thin cigar, then waved the smoke away from her face, and apologised.

'I like the smell of cigar smoke.'

'Anyway, a year or so ago he wrote to me telling me the woman he'd been living with had died. He said if we were ever going to meet – we'd been talking about it for years – it would have to be soon because he didn't have too many years left.'

He put his hand in his pocket and brought out a letter. 'Then I got this just a few weeks ago. It's a different kind of letter. When I read it, it didn't sound like my father at all. There's an air of fear in it, and confusion.'

'He was old.'

66

'I don't mean in that way. He was frightened. Terrified. Apparently the old people around here were being mugged. There was a woman who had lived in the house . . .' He glanced at the spidery writing. 'A Miss Krause. He says she was killed in the gardens outside the house.'

'She was a patient of mine,' Maggie said. 'It isn't true she was mugged.'

'Well, he thought so.'

'You know, if you use this as a basis . . .'

'Bear with me. I'm exploring what *might* have happened. He thought that she was killed by muggers. You were her doctor. You don't think so. I've talked to the police and they don't think so, either. Some time later, my father was badly injured . . .'

'But that was a fall!'

'First of all Miss Krause . . .'

'She died of a—'

'She was going for a walk? In the gardens? On a freezing winter's day?'

That had bothered Maggie, too. She knew that Mrs Mendel believed that Miss Krause had been dragged there. 'Go on.'

'My father slips and falls and injures himself so badly he never comes out of the coma. Okay, so the police say there's no evidence of him being mugged. But what was he doing on the basement steps? He didn't live down there.'

'Going to see Sophie Mendel?'

'The frozen milk he slipped on was up on the pavement. He'd have had to take a few more steps to fall down the basement stairs. And that's if the gate had been left open.'

'What do the police say?'

'They say every elderly person in this part of London – and a lot of other parts – is obsessed by the fear of being mugged.'

'So?'

'At the hospital I saw the doctor who examined him when he was brought in. He said the bruising was compatible with a fall on concrete steps. But it was also compatible with blows.'

She did not want to follow his thinking down that road. If she believed that the Crimea was rife with this kind of violence; if she allowed herself to believe what she feared *could* be true; how would she herself feel going out at night to visit her patients? Would she begin to make excuses? When they telephoned in distress and pain, would she say, 'Take a couple of aspirins and I'll see you in the morning?' Would she begin to take chances with people's lives because she herself was frightened?

'Miss Krause died of a heart attack,' she said firmly.

He said, 'According to a report I read in the local paper, her pocket-book was missing. It must have had money in it.'

'The police said it must have been taken after she died. I don't think there was anything missing from your father's pockets, was there?'

'Not that I know of.'

Abruptly she said, 'You like making mysteries.'

'What does that mean?'

'I saw you at the hospital and you denied it.'

He frowned. 'I denied it?'

She named the day and time. 'You said you'd been seeing the sights. "Rubber-necking" was the word you used.'

He did a mental calculation and then nodded. 'Yes, I did go to the hospital that afternoon, but I didn't see my father. They told me at the desk that he'd had visitors and they thought it unwise anyone else should go in. So I looked for the doctor who'd admitted him.'

She felt much of the tension go. 'We were the visitors,

68

Mrs Mendel and I. You still haven't given me any *real* reason why you believe your father's fall wasn't an accident, nor how it happened.'

'I know that. I can think of all sorts of ways it might have been done. He could have been mugged somewhere else and staggered along and fallen. Perhaps he was going to Mrs Mendel for help. The muggers might have been frightened off before they robbed him. There are several scenarios. I want to find the right one.'

'Suppose you're wrong and it was simply an accident? Look at all the time you've wasted.'

'He was my father. It seems worthwhile to me.'

She heard the anger in his voice, and saw a new dimension in his character.

'Sad, very sad. He was a great man in his way.' Mr Ringham sat back in the taxi, his Homburg on his knees and, as he spoke, turned towards Sophie. She looked frail, almost insubstantial by comparison.

Why is he talking like this, she thought? When Stefan was alive all he wanted was the rent. Never a word. Never a chat.

'Do you believe in precognition, Mrs Mendel? Psychical phenomena?'

She wasn't certain what he meant, and kept silent.

'They say some things have curses on them.'

'Like swearing?' she said.

'No. Not like swearing. I refer to King Tut's tomb. The curse that destroyed those who entered it. And the Hope diamond. The owners all came to unpleasant ends.'

Sophie kept alert. Whatever it was he was talking about she didn't trust, because she didn't trust Mr Ringham. Taxi all this way? Why? And what was he doing anyway at Stefan's funeral?

'There are auras, Mrs Mendel. Ectoplasmic auras.'

69

'What is . . .' She tried to pronounce the word, but could not.

'Ghosts, Mrs Mendel. Spirits. Those who cannot rest.'

'What has that to do with me?'

The taxi went down the Mall and she had a brief view of Buckingham Palace. For a moment it lay under brilliant sunlight, then the shadows of clouds leached out the colour.

'I've always thought that houses absorbed something of their inhabitants,' Mr Ringham said. 'Their auras if you like. You see, I've always thought that houses lived their own lives.'

Sophie shivered slightly.

'First Miss Krause,' he said. 'Then Mr Nedza.'

The taxi emerged from Balaclava Place, crossed Inkerman Street and entered Sebastopol Square.

'Would you like me to come down with you?' Mr Ringham said.

'No! No!'

'Be careful, Mrs Mendel. Be careful where you put your feet. You never know what has spilled on the steps.'

She stared into the taxi. 'Why do you say that? Why?'

'For your own good.'

'What do you know of it?'

'I know that Mr Nedza fell.'

In her agitation she turned away, forgetting to thank him, opened her gate and slowly descended the stairs. She had her glasses on now and peered carefully at every step. There were marks on the two steps where the milk had been, marks where she had scraped away the ice. She heard the taxi accelerate out of the Square, and silence descended again.

She opened her door and locked it behind her. Little light entered her flat so that in a way it was like coming from daylight to dusk. In winter she had to use the lights all the time and this made things more expensive, so she tried not to. But now she needed cheering up: she needed warmth and light. She took off her coat and hat and put them in the bedroom, came back, switched on the light and lit the gas fire.

· 'That's better,' she said to Winston. Then she noticed that the cage was still covered with the old tablecloth she used to keep it dark at night.

'*Ach, mein Liebchen!*' she said, going towards the cage. 'Did I forget to take it off?'

She heard a faint chittering noise of the budgie brushing its beak on the bars.

She took off the tablecloth. 'There! I . . .' The rest of the sentence finished in a half-scream. A great brown rat sprang from side to side in the cage, spilling the water and the birdseed, chittering angrily to itself, its long teeth shining with saliva. On the floor of the cage were some bright green feathers.

'Aaaah!' she said in disgust. '*Liebe Gott!*'

She staggered backwards and collapsed into a chair. The rat paused, looking at her.

'Horrible!' she cried. 'Horrible! Horrible!' She rose. 'And now I do something horrible to you!' There was anger and violence in her tone and her body felt strong again, strong enough to lift the cage from its hook.

She carried it into the bathroom and placed it in the bath. The rat dashed backwards and forwards.

'Now for you!'

The rat lunged at her every time she came near.

'Yes, I know,' she said. 'You would bite me and I would die from your disease. So . . .'

She turned on the taps and the water flowed into the bath. Soon it covered the bottom of the cage. Birdseed floated out and so did the green feathers. The water rose higher. The rat began to swim. It swam desperately, bumping into the bars, trying to chew through them with its long teeth. Up and up the water rose and faster and faster the rat swam until finally the water closed over the top of the cage. The tip of its nose broke the surface of the water as it forced its way up through the bars with all its strength, then that, too, was covered and Sophie switched off the taps.

'So,' she said. She stood in the doorway, trembling. Then she went to the sideboard in her living-room and gave herself a glass of the port she kept for visitors.

She left the cage in the bath for nearly an hour and then, with what remained of her strength, she lifted it out, wrapped the dead rat in newspaper and placed it in the rubbish bins outside. She cleaned up the cage and replaced it on its stand. That drained her of the last of her energy and she sat down and stared vacantly at nothing.

Slowly her eyes focused on the cage again. The bird had been the focal point of her life for so long and she had talked to it so many times that now, even uninhabited, the cage still seemed to have life.

'Poor Winston,' she said, hating herself for having left the bird at risk.

But had she? She could have sworn that she had closed the little door when she had given Winston his water that morning. Was her memory playing tricks? If she *had* given him water, why had she put the cover back on?

The cage could not help her. It hung from its hook on the chromium stand, an enigma, empty, accusatory.

And how had the rat got there? She rose and touched the slippery chromium. 'Impossible!' she said.

It could not have come any other way: not from the ceiling, not from the window, not from the wall, from the mantelpiece, from the top of a chair.

There was only one way for a rat to reach the cage and that was to climb the thin chromium-plated pole that supported it. Then it would have had to open the door.

She was no expert on how rats climbed, but she was certain that no living animal except a monkey could have climbed that pole. And that is what really frightened her. Because if it had not climbed the pole, how had it got into the cage?

The gas fire hissed and bubbled, but she did not hear it. She was listening to the house.

9

'She knew your father for forty years,' Maggie said as she and Seago walked into Sebastopol Square.

'That's just about the whole of his life after he left Poland.'

An icy wind blew along Inkerman Street from Balaclava Place and into the Square, moving the dark fingers of the plane trees against the grey sky.

'And she's the one who found him,' Maggie said.

They went down the basement steps to Sophie's flat. Maggie knocked at the door and called out, 'It's me, Mrs Mendel. Margaret Hollis.'

There was a pause and at first she thought Sophie must be out. But then, so close to her that she realised the old lady was standing directly on the other side of the door, came the voice: '*Doctor* Hollis?'

'Yes. Doctor Hollis. I'd like to see you for a moment.'

'I don't need no doctor.'

'It's about Mr Nedza.'

They heard a bolt being drawn and the chain come off and the key turning in the lock.

'I've brought someone to see you,' Maggie said, stepping into the dimly lit flat. Bill Seago hunched his shoulders as he entered the door. Everything seemed much smaller when he straightened up.

Sophie looked at him closely. 'The funeral,' she said.

'This is Mr Nedza's son,' Maggie said.

'Stefan never had no son.'

'Yes he did, Mrs Mendel,' Bill said. 'From his first wife. The one who died.'

He told her briefly what had happened and saw confusion on her face. 'A son? A son?' she said finally, accepting it. 'I never knew that. But why not? With all his ladies, why not?'

She made them sit down and began to bustle about in the kitchen. 'I make tea.'

'Please don't bother.'

'For Stefan's son? What bother?'

Maggie went back into the living-room. 'You're honoured. She's never made tea for me.'

Sophie bustled back with a lacy tablecloth and then brought out her best china from the cabinet. She smiled at Seago. 'Such a wonderful thing – a son.'

They drank the tea and nibbled at biscuits that were pliable with age and damp.

Sophie said, 'So *lucky* to have a son!'

'I guess I was lucky to have a father. The sad thing was we never met.' He told her briefly about the letters, then about the last one he had received a few weeks ago and which had caused him to come to England. 'You knew him better than anyone: would you say he was frightened?'

She chewed patiently on a biscuit. 'He was an old man,' she said finally. 'Of course he was frightened. We are all frightened. But no one believes us!' She looked penetratingly at Maggie. 'He wanted to leave. To live in the country.'

'He mentioned that in a letter,' Bill said. 'He said the country was safer.'

'But why was he afraid? Why so suddenly?' Maggie said.

'One day you'll be afraid,' Sophie said, and for a second Maggie seemed to look through a door into a bleak, cold wasteland.

They talked about Stefan as they finished their tea, Bill

Seago probing, asking about his father's life, what he did, how he had planned to pay for this new country living.

Finally Sophie said, 'Your father was like that. Always something. I never paid no attention.'

As they rose to go, Bill said, 'I have his house-key. I'll have to go through his things. But I'll let you know when I come.'

Maggie saw the empty birdcage. It had been pushed into a dark corner. 'Where's your budgie?' she said. 'I hope nothing . . .'

'He died,' Sophie said.

'I'm sorry. You'll miss him.' Bill climbed the steps onto street level. 'Are you all right? How are the eyes?' Sophie shrugged. 'I wish you'd see the specialist again. Would you?'

'Maybe.'

'When?'

'One day.'

There was only so much you could do, Maggie thought. She joined Bill. He was looking up at the old houses. 'What a place to live,' he said.

'I've asked her over and over to move. She won't.'

'I suppose when you get old your territory becomes even more important.'

'Territory?'

'Oh, sure. We're just as territorial as animals.' He turned and crossed the street, stopping near the gate leading into the Square gardens. 'Was this where Miss Krause died?'

'Yes.'

He looked at the broken gate, the unkempt privet-hedge, the rusty stop-netting, the old mattresses and tyres, the weeds and the grass and she saw the Square through his eyes, and felt ashamed. As though reading her thoughts, he said, 'We've got places like this, too. Even worse. Show me where it happened.'

They went through the gate onto what had once been

76

a gravel path but which was now a rutted track covered in weeds. There was an old bench near the tennis court. They stopped about thirty feet away. Maggie said, 'I think this is about where she was found.' He walked on, stared at the bench, turned back towards her. 'She could have been making for the bench,' Maggie said. 'The cardiac problem might have started developing on the pavement.'

'I thought heart attacks were sudden.'

'They don't have to be. If it had started in the street she would have seen the bench – or known about it, she must have passed by here every day. It's natural that she would have made for it. If she'd been dragged here there would have been tracks.'

'That's the first thing I asked the police. There weren't any,' he said.

'There you are, then.'

'She could have been carried. They say she was small and light.'

He wandered off towards the far end of the gardens. There was a stubborn streak in him, she thought, and she wondered about his wife. Ex-wife. Stella. Why had she not gone to live with him in those faraway places? If Alec had been a medical missionary, would she, Maggie, have gone with him to live in deserts or in slums? Difficult for some-one who had never been tested to judge, she thought.

The wind was cold and she began to congeal. She watched him disappear behind an overgrown shrubbery. On the far side of the court was the old tennis hut. She walked towards it. At least she would be able to get out of the wind. Once it had stood among neatly clipped box-hedges with a wall of shrubs behind it, giving it privacy from the houses on the other side of the Square. Now the rhododendrons and elaeagnus and shrub roses had grown out of all control.

The hut itself was open to the sky, with only three of the walls remaining. The floorboards were rotten, broken in parts, and it, too, had been used as a rubbish dump. She walked round to shelter between the shrubs and the rear walls of the hut. As she turned the corner she saw a group of youths with shaven heads. One had his nose buried in a plastic bag. There were four of them. Skinheads. She had seen them before.

The youth with his nose in the bag lifted his head and stared at her, and she had a sudden glimpse of vacant madness. She turned to go back, but one of them blocked her path. He had cold grey eyes and a face that was blank of expression. The others closed around her.

'I know you,' she said to the boy with grey eyes.

He stared at her.

She searched her memory for a name but all she could see was a vandalised block of council flats; graffiti everywhere. She had been helping out because Alec was ill and the telephone call had sounded urgent. She'd gone up to a flat on the fifth floor. There was a woman lying in a diabetic coma. Maggie remembered the boy standing next to the bed. He had stared at her like an animal guarding its kin. It had been too late to save the mother. The boy had been taken into care. When was that? Three or four years ago? He would be about fourteen now.

'I remember you,' she said again.

'Got any fags?' one of the youths said.

Another said, 'Give us some money.' He was holding an expensive ghetto-blaster. He put his other hand on her shoulder-bag. Suddenly she seemed a long way from any form of civilisation.

She could only see three of them. She half-turned and felt a jerk on the bag. She stepped back, pushing herself against the wooden wall so that no one could get behind her.

'I'm a doctor,' she said.

The leader nodded. She thought, Doctors, nurses and midwives were said to have a certain immunity.

'I hate doctors,' he said.

She moved along the wall, trying to get past the tangle of shrubs so that she could see Bill. They crowded her and she felt another tug on her bag. She thought of screaming. And then she felt angry. Why should *they* make *her* scream?

'Is this what you did to Miss Krause?' she said.

'Who's Miss Krause?' the leader said.

'Is this what you did? Try to rob her? Frighten her to death?'

'You accusing us?'

One of the boys said, 'Give us some money or we'll do you.'

She could feel their hands on her now, on her bag and under her coat.

Then everything seemed to stop. She and the boys looked up. Bill Seago was regarding them from a distance of about ten feet.

The youths fell back a few paces. Again the metaphor flashed through her mind of jackals and a lion. One of the boys held something in his hand. It glinted in the cold grey light. A sharpened screwdriver.

'You all right?' Bill said.

She moved towards him. 'Fine. We were talking. I thought I knew one of them.'

'And did you?'

She turned. The boys waited. He was so big, she thought, but they were so many.

'No,' she said. 'No, I didn't.'

He took a couple of steps backward, then turned. He took her arm and they walked round the tennis court to the gate.

'Not too fast,' he said. 'Act normal. Don't give them the satisfaction.'

'Mr Ringham to see Mr Deacon.'

Miss Marriner, the typist-receptionist, looked up at the stirring sight of Mr Ringham in his long black overcoat with the frogging at the buttonholes, the astrakhan collar and Homburg hat. At first she thought it was Sidney Greenstreet, stepped out of *The Maltese Falcon*. She was thin and had a bad skin and watched a lot of movies on television.

'Sorry. Who?'

'Mr Ringham of Hubert Ringham Associates.' 'Associates' was one of his little embellishments. It looked good on his cards. 'Hubert Ringham Associates. Rent and Debt Collectors. Discretion Our Watchword.'

The receptionist consulted her diary and in a few moments he was shown into Kenneth Deacon's office. It was the first time he had been there. His impression was of expensive greenery and cool colours, everything modern, glass and tubular steel. On the wall behind Deacon's desk was a photograph of his wife and children, taken a year or so before she died. Mr Ringham remembered Edna. Her father had once owned an electrical shop in Pimlico. Before the war he had been nothing more than a glorified repair man; later, with the TV, radio and cassette boom, he had expanded into something big.

Kenneth was wearing a dark chalk-striped suit, white shirt and silk Paisley tie. For a moment he went on working, leaving Mr Ringham marooned in the middle of the room. Finally he looked up and motioned to a plain wooden chair. Ever since he had seen Hubert Ringham's name on the diary he had been wondering what he wanted, and wondering what his own attitude should be. He had thought of cancelling, but his curiosity had won.

'Well, Ringham, what can I do for you?'

'Ringham? Ringham, is it?'

'What should I call you?'

'You used to call me Hubert.'

'That was bef . . . that was a long time ago.'

'I can remember when I used to come and fetch you from school. It wasn't Ringham then. Oh no. It was, Hubert will you buy me a milkshake? Hubert will you buy me some chocolate?'

'As I say, it was a long time ago.'

'Some of us don't forget so easily,' Mr Ringham said. 'That's what makes me sad. We had a relationship once. After your mum died. You. Your father. And me.'

'You were my father's clerk.'

'Managing clerk!'

'All right, managing clerk. You worked for my father. That's all the relationship we had. He asked you to fetch me from school and take me to the cinema sometimes because he didn't have the time. Nothing more.'

'We were friends.'

Kenneth looked down at his desk. He wondered again what the old fake wanted. You'd think he was someone grand, important, the way he carried on. Always seemed to be acting someone else; a bit larger than life. Yet there was also something dangerous about Mr Ringham. 'Well?' Kenneth said.

'I've got a business proposition to put to you.'

'Go on.'

'What if I was to say to you, Kenneth, that I knew of property not more than a few stones' throw from where we're sitting now, prime sites, which could be had cheaply for development.'

'Sitting tenants,' Kenneth said.

'I beg your pardon?'

'You said what would I say if you told me you could lay your hands on cheap property in this area. The only cheap property is either falling down or has sitting tenants.'

Mr Ringham blinked. 'You may be right.'

'Of course I'm right.'

81

'Let's, for argument's sake, say you are. And if I tell you I know how to get property free of all encumbrances, what would you say then?'

Kenneth looked at him for a long moment and then said, 'I'm not sure I'm hearing you correctly, Ringham. What are you telling me this for?'

'Partnership, Kenneth.'

'You mean, like the partnership you had with my father?'

'No, no, that was just . . .' Mr Ringham waved his hand to dismiss it.

'Anyway, how are you going to get sitting tenants out? Rehouse them?'

'There are other ways.'

'And you want me to put up the money, is that it?'

'I find the properties. I get rid of the encumbrances. You put up the money.'

'Getting rid of the encumbrances, as you put it – that's criminal. You've already been inside twice.'

'Once.'

'Twice.'

'You could hardly call the first time anything. You could hardly call *that* criminal. She *looked* eighteen.'

'It's what the judge called it.'

'Look . . .' Mr Ringham began.

'I don't want to discuss it. And I don't want you coming here.'

'I could come to your house. We could talk there.'

'No!'

Ah, thought Mr Ringham, touched him there in a soft spot. For years now he had watched Kenneth go out of his way to avoid him. Especially with his daughter. Once he had crossed the road with Joan and pretended to be absorbed by a shop window. Mr Ringham had crossed, too, and the three of them had stared for a minute or more at a window filled with bras and undies and corsets. Mr

Ringham had turned and caught the little girl's eye, had given an elaborate wink, then turned away.

'I don't want you coming to my house,' Kenneth said.

Other thoughts began to slide into Mr Ringham's mind.

10

'Just thinking about it makes my skin crawl.' Maggie poured Seago a whisky and carried it over to him. He was sitting in a corner of her big sofa, his arm stretched out in his familiar pose, hand hanging down, relaxed.

'You're not having one?' he said.

'I'm on call.' She poured herself a glass of Perrier with lemon and ice. She gave an uncontrolled shiver. 'I've never been happier to see anyone.'

'That's what knights in shining armour always like to hear.'

'It's no joke. I was absolutely terrified.' She sat on the arm of a chair.

'I wasn't so brave myself. I didn't know about this solvent thing. They sniff it in plastic bags, is that it?' She nodded. 'It's new to me. We've got every drug you've ever heard of and a whole bunch you haven't. But I guess I missed the solvent kick.'

'It's reached epidemic proportions here. Especially up north. Children mainly. Of course, some of them graduate to the harder drugs.'

'Have you thought of that kid's name yet?'

She shook her head. 'I could go back through Alec's files. They're downstairs.'

'Knowing his name could help. They hang around the

Square. Miss Krause died there. So did my father. There could be a connection.'

They went on picking at the subject, examining those few frightening moments in the garden from every angle. She had felt upset for much of the day, and running through her reaction, like an unbroken thread, was her gratitude to Bill. She would never forget the feeling of those hands under her coat, the mad, drugged eyes, the panic that had gripped her. And then the way the boys had turned and looked at the big man who was watching them in silence.

She poured him another drink and sat on the corner of the coffee-table, perching nervously, like a bird.

He said, 'What are you planning to do about dinner?'

'I hadn't thought.'

'Can you go out when you're on call?'

She pointed to her handbag. 'I have a bleeper. It's all right as long as I don't go too far. And I have a phone in the car.'

'How about it then?'

She went to the window and shaded the glass with her hands. A wind was blowing along the empty street. Diagonally across the road she could see the lighted windows of a telephone booth, and further along the pool of light shed by the windows of S. Flower and Son. They were the only two islands of warmth. For the rest, the plane trees moved in the wind and paper blew along the pavements. She shivered again with the memory of what had happened that day.

She turned back to the room and said, 'I used to cook Chinese for . . .' She paused.

'Alec?'

'Yes.'

'I could help you.'

She gave him a list for the nearby supermarket and he was back in fifteen minutes. She had always thought her kitchen was fair-sized; now it seemed small. They chopped up the chicken breasts and squeezed the lemons; she found the wok, the soy, the cornflour and sherry. They had been in the cupboard, unused since Alec's death. Suspended, like herself.

They worked quickly, not talking much, but she found herself, for the first time in many months, feeling a positive sense of enjoyment as she cooked. They ate in the sitting-room. When they finished he offered to help wash up, but she told him the cleaning woman came in the morning, and they settled down with their coffee.

He resumed what she now thought of as 'his place' in the corner of the sofa. The coffee-cup looked ridiculously small in his hand. She was filled with nervous tension, and stood at the window, drinking her coffee.

'You're hovering,' he said. 'Why don't you relax?' He patted the sofa next to him.

She decided that might be too dangerous and made for a chair. Halfway there she thought that might embarrass both of them and completed a kind of semi-circle to find herself on the sofa after all, aware of his arm behind her.

There was a slight, uneasy pause and she said, 'What are you going to do now?'

'You mean at this very moment?'

'About your father?'

'Finished your coffee?'

She had been holding onto the cup like a kind of life-belt, now she surrendered it to him. He put it with his own on the table.

'Try to find answers,' he said.

She felt his fingers on her hair, lightly fretting the ends. She knew what was about to happen and part of her wanted it and another part was afraid. It would complicate her life. And then it happened. He flexed the muscles in his arm and she found herself impelled towards him.

'I don't think this is a good . . .' she began.

He kissed her. There was nothing tentative about it. It was powerful, almost brutal. Alec had been a gentle lover. She had enjoyed sex with him but it had never been at the centre of their relationship. And Kenneth hardly counted. Now, as Seago kissed her, nerve endings felt scraped and raw as though she had gripped a wire through which a current was passing. Huge physical changes suddenly took place in her body, but her doctor's analytical mind was blurred by feelings she had not experienced before. She found herself gripping the back of his neck, felt her fingers lock, then she was pulling him down on top of her. She felt buttons come loose, his hands were on her naked skin. She made love with an abandon and ferocity that left her shaken and somewhat disorientated.

Slowly the room reassembled itself. She realised that her clothing, part on the floor, part still on her body, was mainly around her waist. Bill's weight was on top of her. She felt crushed by him, but was too drained to move him. He rolled away from her, then turned and kissed her again. 'It's a long time since I interfered with anyone on an ottoman,' he said.

She began to laugh. He joined her. Their laughter filled the room.

'Give me a minute,' she said, and gathered up her clothing. In a few moments she was back from the bedroom, wearing her long caftan and brushing her hair.

'At this point I become very English,' she said, 'and say, "A little more coffee?"'

He took her hand and kissed it. 'You don't smoke cigars, do you?'

She started to speak, then stopped herself. It wasn't the moment to mention Alec's name.

The telephone rang. She looked at her watch. It was almost ten o'clock. Mentally she quickly went through the names and faces of patients who might be needing her.

'Let it ring,' he said.

'I can't.'

He rose and went to the window while she crossed the room and picked up the telephone. 'Dr Hollis,' she said. There was silence. 'Hello?' She thought she heard faint breathing. 'Hello? This is Doctor Hollis?' Seago was watching her. She raised her shoulders. 'Hello?' she said again, then put the receiver down. 'Maybe it was a wrong number.'

In the call-box at the corner of Balaclava Place, Kenneth Deacon replaced the phone and watched her windows. Both top floors of the house were glowing with light. He had seen what he thought he might see, two figures in her sitting-room. One was Margaret herself, the other was the big American who had been walking with her, the man to whom he had rented the flat.

'Input?' Mrs Flower said. 'Why do they call it input? You sure?'

''Course I'm sure,' Ronnie said.

'But in means in. It's what comes in.'

'That's where you're wrong. In means out and out means in.'

They were at the dining-room table in one of the rooms above the shop, doing their VAT returns.

'It's all this Common Market,' Mrs Flower said. 'And the new money.'

'It hasn't been new for years,' Ronnie said. 'We went decimal years ago. You know that. And it's easier. Stands to reason, all you do is move the decimal point.'

'I liked the old money. Pounds, shillings and pence. You knew what a bob was. And half-a-crown. Not like this money.'

The table was a mass of papers. It was a ritual they went through once a month: Mrs Flower complaining,

Ronnie explaining. He leaned back in his chair and said, 'Well, we ain't done too badly this month.'

He pushed a piece of paper across the table and indicated the total with his index finger.

'I ain't got my glasses,' she said.

He leaned back and picked them off the sideboard and gave them to her. She put them on grudgingly. He smiled to himself. She looked at the total for some time, then said, 'We could have done better. You ordered too many of them model planes.' She waved her large hand in the direction of the door through which the piles of boxes could be seen. 'They ain't on sale or return.'

'We'll sell them.'

'When?'

'Next Christmas, if we have to wait that long.'

They bickered on for another half-hour. It was a habit. He passed her a ballpoint pen. 'Sign there.' He indicated the bottom of a printed form. 'And there.' He moved papers rapidly between himself and his mother.

'You sure?'

''Course I'm sure. You don't want to go to prison, do you?'

'You always say that. And I'm always signing things.'

'Look, do you want me to tell you how VAT works? You want me to sit down right now and tell you? Explain everything from top to bottom?'

Mrs Flower was defeated. 'No.'

''Cause if you do, I will. I'll spend the whole night and we'll get the Inspector down and let him explain it too. First of all, we'll explain why inputs are outputs and outputs are inputs.'

Mrs Flower signed where he indicated. She was cowed for a moment, humbled by Ronnie's grasp of fiscal affairs.

She's like a bleedin' peasant, he thought. One of them French peasants in the movies. But you had to hand it to her. She'd done pretty well for herself considering what she started with.

As she signed the various forms he looked at her and his mouth turned down in distaste. To think he could have come out of that! He could barely remember his father, but he had a sudden vision, as he sometimes did, of him astride this percheron. Christ, he thought, it didn't seem possible. He gathered up the papers, put some in a box-file, others in envelopes.

'Well, that's done,' he said.

Mrs Flower didn't like her evenings to be dominated by Ronnie. His father hadn't dominated her and *he* wasn't going to. And yet she just didn't understand and she knew she never would understand, no matter how often he explained it. So once a month she put up with it. Now that it was over she turned viciously on him and said, 'You better sell those model aircraft otherwise I'll stop it off your money.'

She would, too, he thought, bloody old bitch. She'd done it several times in the past. Treating him like a school-boy. Well, that wasn't going to last much longer.

He put away the file and gummed down the envelopes and rose.

'Where're you going?' she said.

'Out.'

'At this time of night? And what about me?'

'You've got the telly.'

He picked up his coat and the VAT envelopes and went out into the night. There were few people about. It was bitterly cold, with a wind out of Russia that cut like a blade. He posted the envelopes at the corner box and as he did so, he saw a figure leave the telephone-box and come along the pavement towards him.

'Evening, Mr Deacon.'

'Oh, hello, Ronnie.' Kenneth made a move to pass, but Ronnie blocked the way.

'I got to see you,' Ronnie said.

'Oh?'

'On business.'

He expected Deacon's eyes to show more interest, instead they seemed angry and unfocused.

'Any time,' Deacon said, and walked past him.

Ronnie frowned, then went on his way. He stopped at one of the houses in Inkerman Street and rang the bell.

'Yes?' said Denise's voice on the door-phone. 'Who is it?'

'It's me, Ronnie.'

'What do you want?'

'I want to come up.'

'Not tonight.'

'I got some news.'

'What sort of news?'

'Can't stand here in the street shouting it.'

'Oh, all right.' The lock buzzed and the door opened.

Her room, pink and warm, was the place Ronnie wanted most to be. It smelled of her talc and her perfume and her body. Heady provocative smells. And Denise herself was looking provocative. She was wearing a silky nightdress under her kimono.

'Look at the time!' she said. 'Well, go on, what's all this news?'

He noticed that her body bulged, but it did so in the places Ronnie most liked women to bulge. He put his hand on her breast, but she twisted away. 'Enough of that!'

'Come on, Denise.'

'You can't just come barging in here whenever you like.'

'Look!' From his coat pocket he brought out a small box of chocolates. There had been a promotion and the rep had given him this one free.

Her eyes lit up. Delicately, with thumb and fore-finger, she took out a chocolate and popped it into her mouth.

'That's very nice, Ronnie. Very nice.'

She patted the bed beside her and his spirits rose. You could never tell with Denise.

'April,' he said.

'April what?'

'That's when we go. You and me.'

'You're still on about that!'

'True. April. The end of.'

'Who?'

'Just you and me. Special flight. All laid on for people looking for property.'

She stopped chewing. 'You mean it?'

'Torremolinos, here we come!'

'Just the two of us?'

'Just the two of us.'

11

'For you,' Bill Seago said.

The budgerigar was in a small wicker carrying-cage. Mrs Mendel came closer and stared at it. Where Winston had been green, this one was blue. 'Why?' she said.

'I thought you'd like it.'

'No! No!' She started back.

'What's wrong?' It was the last reaction he had expected. She looked ashen.

'You want it should die too? You want it should be eaten?'

He stood, holding the small cage, not understanding. 'There's no problem, I'll take it back. It came from the shop on the corner,' he said. 'Is there anything you'd rather have? I just thought, well, company.'

Slowly she shook her head. 'You didn't see it.'

'What?'

'In the cage.'

'What was in the cage, Mrs Mendel?'

'Better you don't ask.'

'Tell me.'

'Stefan's son,' she said, as though it was a kind of guarantee. She switched on the middle light and pointed to the empty cage that stood in the corner. 'Tell me how it is possible. How something could have climbed the pole.'

'What?'

'A rat.'

'A rat climbed the pole?'

'And opened the door and killed the bird and put the cover on.'

He crossed to the cage and opened the little door and put in the blue budgie. 'Just temporarily,' he said. 'Now tell me about it.'

She told him. And about the milk on the steps. And she told him again about Miss Krause and about how she had found his father.

'Have you got any enemies?' he said. 'Is there someone who hates you?'

'God knows. You want some tea?'

'I came to look over my father's things. I'll go up.'

'I come with you.'

She led him up the narrow staircase from the kitchen.

'Who used to live here?' he said as they reached the ground floor.

'Lily Oppenheimer.'

'She dead too?'

'In the old people's home.'

They went into Stefan's flat on the first floor. He peered into the bathroom and kitchen, not knowing what he was looking for, just getting a sense of the old man he had met only on his death-bed. Sophie was standing in the bed-sitting room. 'Your father was a tidy man,' she said.

In the wardrobe the clothes hung neatly on their hangers and he saw the Polish Air Force uniform. They would have to go to a junk-shop now.

'Is there anything you want?' he said. 'I'm going to have to get rid of all this. If there's anything you like, take it.'

'Thanks, but no thanks. I got too much already. When they come to take me away, they . . .'

He was inspecting the wardrobe. 'You didn't hear anything? Like furniture being moved?'

Only the house, she thought. Only the wind in the

empty rooms. Only the timbers moving and straining as though talking to her. How could she explain that to him? It was difficult enough to explain to herself. 'I don't know,' she said.

'You'd know if you'd heard it.' Then he said. 'Why do you stay here, Mrs Mendel?'

'You, too!'

'It's no place for an old person.'

'Stefan's son should say that!'

'What's that got to do with it?'

'Everybody tries to get me out and Stefan too, and Lily and Miss Krause!'

'Why should I want to get you out except for your own good? I know I wouldn't live here.'

'How can you know? You're a baby! A young man.'

'It's a long time since I was called a young man, but thanks.'

They closed the door and locked it and went back to her basement. The moment they opened the door they heard the noises of the budgie.

'It's enjoying itself,' he said. 'Why don't you keep it for a few days? If you don't want it then, I'll take it back. But don't be frightened.'

'Why do you say that?'

'I mean it. I'm going to be around for a while.'

'Why?'

'Because there are things that don't add up.'

'You want some tea?'

'All right.'

She made them a pot and they sat together. He said, 'I told you I had a letter from my father a couple of weeks ago. He was worried and seemed to be frightened. He talked about leaving here and going to live in the country because it was safer.'

'*Ja.* That was his rubbish. Excuse me I should say that about your father, but I knew him.'

'Better than I did.' Then he said, 'Where was he getting the money from?'

'There was no money.'

'There was *something*. It was in the letter. He said there was something that was going to make a difference to his life.'

She shook her head.

'I don't suppose we'll ever know now,' he said. 'Unless there are papers. Something like that.'

'I got something,' she said. 'No, no, not important. Not what you're looking for. A bill. Something like that.'

'For my father?'

'*Ja*. When he was in the hospital.'

She went into her bedroom, came back a minute later. 'It ain't in my coat.'

'In a drawer?'

'Maybe.'

She stood in the centre of the room, thinking.

'You remember what you were wearing? You wouldn't wear a coat indoors, would you?'

'Ah!' She fetched her apron from the kitchen and felt in the big pocket. Her hand came out with the letter. He tore it open. It was just a few lines long.

'It's from a place called Greeley's.'

'Jewellers. Down by Victoria Station.'

He passed it to her, but she shook her head. 'I have to find my other glasses.'

' "Dear Sir" ' he read. ' "We regret our inability to appraise the item in the time allowed, but such work is done by experts and we would not be fulfilling our obligation to our customers if care was not taken. Should you change your mind and wish us to carry out the work, we would be only too pleased. Yours faithfully." And then the signature. Someone called S. Hopkirk (Miss).'

'He was seen at Greeley's,' she said. 'He never told me.'

'What would he be doing at a jeweller's? What item?'

'You want more tea?'

'No, thanks. I'll check this out.'

'Your father . . . maybe . . .'

'What?'

'When you get old, things change. Maybe it was . . .'
She tapped her head. 'Maybe it was only here. Only in
the mind.'

'There's the letter.'

'That's true.'

He was about to leave when he had another thought.
'You all got old here, I mean in these two houses,
didn't you?'

'*Ja.*'

'Tell me about the others. Tell me what happened
to them.'

Maggie flicked the intercom in her surgery and heard
Mrs Castle answer. 'That the lot?'

'So far.'

She looked at her watch. 'Off you go then,' she said.

She rose and went to the window. The mist had come
back and the street-lights were haloed by moisture. She
stared out at Balaclava Place and Inkerman Street and
the mouth of Sebastopol Square, but she saw nothing
except the furniture of her own mind. Bill had been out
all day; at least, she hadn't heard him in the house, and
this had given her time to reflect. She knew herself too
well not to realise the dangers ahead. Whatever chemistry
was supposed to work between man and woman quite
clearly worked between herself and Bill. But there were
other things as well: a sense of belonging, of common
interests, of friendship and respect; above all, her longing
to be in his company. Put these together with the physical
aspect, and it was called love. She could easily see herself
falling in love with him, which was why she needed to
put a check on the situation right now. To suffer again a

97

similarly traumatic experience as she had done on Alec's death didn't bear contemplation.

Bill had already made his position clear. He was a man of the world's great empty spaces. Soon he'd pack his bags and go and her life would be even emptier than it had been.

She turned away from the window, paused briefly as she made her final decision, then picked up the phone and dialled.

It was answered almost immediately.

'Kenneth?' she said.

'Hello, stranger.'

'Do you know what day it is?'

'Of course. Where would you like to eat?'

'Anywhere.'

'I'll think of somewhere. Give me an hour.'

She put the receiver down. 'Good girl,' she said out loud to herself.

She locked the surgery and went upstairs, showered and was dressing when her phone rang.

A voice said, 'This is your tenant.'

'Hello Bill.'

'I heard you come upstairs. It's Thursday and you're not on call. Is that right?'

'Yes, it is, but . . .'

'But me no buts, as the fellow said. I read in the *Standard* about a Japanese restaurant in Kensington. Is that far?'

'No, not really, but . . .'

'There you go again,' he said.

'Look, I've got a . . . date,' she said. The word dropped into the atmosphere fully clothed in inverted commas, wrenched bodily from an old movie.

'A date?'

He made it sound as if it was something new and barely comprehensible.

'Yes.'

'Man?'

'Yes.'

'Put him off.'

'I can't, Bill.'

'I'll put him off.' He was trying to keep everything light.

'It's not possible,' she said.

There was a pause and then his voice changed its timbre. 'Okay. Well, have a good time. See you.'

She heard the click of the receiver and stood looking at her own. 'Yes, see you,' she said to the silent line.

'I thought you might have forgotten, or you were too busy,' Kenneth said.

'Don't be silly.'

They were at a Spanish restaurant in Soho. Kenneth was wearing a black velvet jacket, open-necked white shirt, gold chain round his neck and a gold bracelet on his left wrist. She realised that she had never seen him dressed like this before; that he had made a special effort.

They were making a whole meal of *tapas* and her concentration was fixed on small dishes containing *pinchitas* and *gambas* and *guacamole* and some others she did not recognise. They ate, and drank a *rioja*, and Kenneth talked about money. He was telling her about a development south of the river in which he had an interest. How much the land was per square foot, how many storeys you had to build to make it worth while and how planning authorities were being difficult and extra money had to be passed around for the boys.

She only half listened. She had no interest in developments either north or south of the river and didn't like the idea of local government officials being bribed.

'You talk about it as though it's an everyday affair,' she said.

'Why do you think people go into local government?'

'That's very cynical.'

99

'Cynical? D'you really think the world runs on the same ethical lines as the medical profession?' He tore a *pinchita* from its small wooden skewer with his teeth. 'In the real world everyone wants a piece of the cake.'

'Have you been to the Isle of Wight recently?' she asked, to change the subject.

'No, but I've heard about a place that could be interesting. On the hill behind Bonchurch. Marvellous view over the town and the sea. A maisonette, but with a big balcony. They're asking a hundred and fifty thousand freehold. That's ridiculous. I could probably get it for a hundred and thirty. Like to see it?'

'When?'

'You say.'

'I'd have to look at my diary.'

They drove back to Pimlico. The mist was thicker here than in Soho. The interior of the new car should have given her pleasure, but instead she felt hemmed in, almost claustrophobic. She had deliberately telephoned Kenneth because he was safe, because she would never fall in love with him, and there would never be any bruising, any trauma. Now she knew she had been a fool. Her mind touched briefly on – and rejected – the scenario of the next hour.

As he pulled up in front of the house she said, 'I'd ask you up, Kenneth, but . . .'

He turned to look at her, his thin face angry in the orange glow of the street-light. 'But what?'

'It's the first day of my period,' she said. 'And I've got a splitting headache.'

She waited for him to say he was sorry, but it couldn't be helped. Instead he said, 'Why did you ring me then?'

'Because I wanted to see you.'

'I thought there were supposed to be pills you could take.'

'I don't like taking pills.'

100

He opened his mouth to speak, decided against it. She slipped out of the car quickly. 'I'm sorry Kenneth.'

He shrugged, raised his hand briefly and then he put his foot down and the rear tyres screeched on the tarmac as he took off.

She watched the receding rear lights. That's that, she thought. She felt a moment of relief and at the same time a pang of guilt. She'd been fond of Kenneth. He'd been faithful. She had used him. But he had used her too.

She looked up at the house. The lights on the top floor were on. She went up to her own flat, picked up her telephone and dialled.

'This is your landlady,' she said, as she heard Bill's voice. 'I'm back.'

She put the receiver down and stood where she was, hearing his feet move on the floor above. She had made no conscious decision. Sitting with Kenneth in the restaurant she had known what she was going to do. When Bill went back to America, or Africa, or India, or wherever, she would put up with it. She knew it would happen, but she would cope. In the meantime, she'd enjoy every moment she could spend with him.

They lay together on her bed, bodies limp, limbs intertwined. He turned and kissed her on the cheek, his lips lingering. 'We have an old saying in Boston,' he said. 'East, West, bed's best.' She moved, and put her head on his stomach. 'This beats the sofa any day.'

There was silence for a few moments, then he said, 'What about going away, just the two of us?'

'That would be lovely.'

'But.'

'Yes. But.'

'Don't you take holidays in the medical profession?'

'Not until the spring. I've had to arrange a locum. It's

all got to be organised well in advance. What did you have in mind?'

'Somewhere like the Alpes Maritimes or Vienna. Somewhere we could be alone and doing this all the time.'

'It's never as simple as that.'

'I guess not. Anyway, there's this other thing.'

For a moment she had forgotten the other thing, and tried to reject it now as it crowded back into the room with them, intruding, interrupting.

As though picking up her thoughts he said, 'I talked to old Mrs Mendel today.' He told her about the savagery of the budgie's death and she felt slightly queasy. She rose, put on a dressing-gown and said, 'I'll get some coffee.'

She was back in a few minutes. He was lying on his stomach, his head on his folded arms.

'Thank God you don't have hair growing out of your shoulder-blades,' she said. 'I used to know someone who did.' Strange how Kenneth had slipped into the past.

'I shave them,' he said.

For a fraction of a second she believed him, then she laughed. They drank their coffee on the bed. He lay on his side, his eyes brooding as he looked over the top of the steaming mug.

'She told me about the others,' he said.

'What others?'

'The old folk who lived in the two houses.'

'You're still suspicious?'

'Nothing's changed.'

He got off the bed and fumbled in his jacket pocket. He had no false modesty at all, she thought, and imagined him walking round naked in one of those faraway places. He stretched out beside her again and unfolded a piece of paper. 'They all died off or moved away, but when you look at it against what's happened recently there is a kind of pattern.'

'Miss Krause and your father?'

He touched the paper. 'There was something before that. Lily Oppenheimer.'

'Lily? I know her. She's in Pimlico House. She's senile.'

'Mrs Mendel says she had an accident.'

'You mean her wrist? She was getting off a bus. She fell and broke her wrist. It mended perfectly.'

'Mrs Mendel said she never recovered.'

'That's not true.'

'In her mind. She says it was only a matter of weeks before she went into this old folks' home.'

'Even if that were true, I don't see how they were connected.'

'Maybe there isn't a connection, but maybe there is. You call it an accident.'

'You use the word as though it had some sinister connotation. It means precisely the opposite. A random happening.'

'When we have an accident on site we investigate. There's often a logical explanation. Cause and effect. Many times it isn't random, and often it isn't what you think.'

She remembered his father's body upside-down on the steps, the blood welling from his mouth, glistening blackly in the street-lights.

He touched her. 'You're cold.'

'Yes.' She reached for him, forcing her arms under his, holding him close, taking the warmth from his skin.

'As the days lengthen, the cold strengthens,' Mrs Flower said. 'Ain't that what they say?'

Mrs Mendel was picking over potatoes in a box. Mrs Flower watched her disapprovingly. She did not like people to pick over the vegetables.

'Though you'd never know they were lengthening.' She looked through the window at the sky.

Sophie said nothing. She had never liked Mrs Flower, nor Ronnie. He was stacking his boxes of model aircraft. Such a baby, she thought.

'Best King Edwards, those,' Mrs Flower said severely.

'They got eyes,' Sophie said.

'All potatoes got eyes,' Ronnie said.

Sophie carried the potatoes to the counter and Ronnie weighed them. 'That's twenty-seven pence,' he said.

'Ronald would deliver, you know. Save you coming out in the cold. Wouldn't cost you much more and safer in the long run.

'I like to choose,' Sophie said.

'I can see that.' She paused, sighing. 'You wouldn't need to come out.'

'I wouldn't live where you do,' Ronnie said.

Sophie bit back her reply. She wasn't going to discuss her affairs with shop-keepers.

'How's the eyes then?' Mrs Flower said.

'How's the fibrositis?' Sophie said.

They looked at each other.

Mrs Mendel put her mittened fingers into her purse and inspected a coin, then gave it to Ronnie. He waited. Then he said, 'That's only twopence, Mrs Mendel.'

'Oh, sorry, I thought it was one of the pounds.' She identified a fifty-pence piece by its octagonal shape and gave it to him instead.

'There're lovely retirement homes,' he said. 'Three meals a day, nurses, not a worry. Even got their own doctors.'

Sophie collected her change and turned her back on the Flowers. She pushed at the door and went off down the street on her little stick legs, in her long coat, a woollen knitted hat pulled down over her head to cover her ears. As the days lengthen, the cold strengthens, she thought. But the days were not really lengthening. Maybe it was her eyes, but it seemed darker now than on the shortest day. She glanced over at the gardens. Everything was still. She supposed that whoever it was had been in the garden before had been driven out now by the cold. She came to her own house and looked carefully at the staircase that led down to the basement. She could see nothing untoward.

All her life she had been afraid of returning. As a small child at school, if she had been away ill for a week there had been a flutter of apprehension in her stomach on the day she went back. What would have taken place while she was away? What new friendships would have been forged? Would she be hated, excluded, laughed at?

When she had returned to Berlin with Leni she had been afraid of what she might find. She had not been coming home, for the city she knew had vanished. All her fears had been realised. Now it was the same. Each time she left her basement – her lair you could say – it sapped her courage and her will. Each time she made her lonely journey along the dangerous pavements of Sebastopol Square and Inkerman Street she was faced with the necessity of returning; of wondering whether she had remembered to lock up. Eyesight and memory; memory and eyesight. One received the image, the other stored it. Now both were breaking down.

She unlocked the door and entered the flat. It was a kind of no-man's-land for those few seconds until she had switched on the lights and relocked the door.

'I am home again,' she told the budgie. For the first few days she had ignored the bird, except for giving it water and seed. But the very act of accepting that responsibility had changed her attitude. She needed something to love. It had a different personality from Winston, was more alert, more flighty. If it escaped from the cage during cleaning it buzzed about the room like a wasp, clearly enjoying itself, and it was an effort to catch it again. Once it nearly escaped through the top of her window and out into the London air.

'*Ja, liebchen.*' She put a finger through the bars of the cage. 'I still have no name for you. You don't make noises like Winston. Maybe even you're a girl.' She sprinkled seed on the bottom of the cage from a small packet she had bought at the Flowers' shop. 'There, enjoy yourself.'

She thought of Bill Seago. Such a big man to bring her such a little bird. Stefan's son. And thinking of Stefan she wondered again about Greely's. What had the old man done that time? What new rubbish was that of his?

The telephone rang. It was a startling moment, for Sophie almost never received a telephone call. There was no one to telephone her. Occasionally, like anyone else, she answered a wrong number. But no one phoned her to say, 'Hello, Sophie, how are you? Come and have tea. Come and have dinner.'

She picked up the receiver and heard the laughter. It seemed far away. 'Hello,' she said. There was silence, and then the laugh came again.

Once she had received obscene telephone calls in Berlin before she was married. It had been a miserable experience and she had only endured it for a week before she'd had her number changed.

'Hello?' she said again. And again there was a ripple of soft laughter.

She was cold and she was afraid and she put down the telephone and stood by it, trembling. And then she heard the laughter again and knew it wasn't coming from the telephone. It seemed to be coming from the very walls of her flat.

12

'You sure?' Denise said, as she slowed and the car dipped into a large pothole in the unmade road.

'Yeah,' Ronnie said. 'I think so.'

'This road don't look like it's going anywhere.'

They were in the wilds of Surrey. They had come off the motorway and plunged into a series of secondary roads that became tertiary, finally petering out in lanes and hedgerows and fields and overgrown hawthorn, great drippy hedges of rhododendron until even the tarmac had stopped and they were on a muddy track. Ronnie had a map on his knees.

'I *hate* the country,' Denise said broodingly as leaves brushed the sides of the car. 'And that's where you want to live.'

'Me? In the country? Spain's different. All them hot countries is different. It's, well, I dunno, you just . . . it's grass and olive-trees and houses with red tiles. It's not this sort of country. Not wet country.'

'Like a wet desert,' she said.

They came to a pair of gates sagging on their posts. A newly painted sign at the side of the road said, 'Byde-a-Wee Retirement Home.' Next to it, where it had been flung against the hedge, faded now and broken, was the sign which it had replaced. It read 'Tyger Tim Kennels and Cattery'.

They continued along the unmade road past what had

once been a series of kennels and eventually came to a 1950's bungalow of violent red brick to which an extension had been added at some later date. They parked along the side of the house, saw several old people sitting in chairs by windows, fast asleep. Sometime in the not too distant past an attempt had been made at a garden. Several beds running along the sides of the house had been planted with marigolds, but they were brown and dead now in the winter cold.

'You want me to come with you?' Denise said.

'No.' He took with him a small briefcase and went to the front door. He was let in by a person whose sex was not immediately apparent. He/she was about six feet tall, burly, with what were either small female breasts or a fat masculine chest. Hair hung down almost to the shoulders.

'I'm Mrs Jolliffe,' she said. 'You must be Mr Flower. Come in, come in.' He thought she might be about fifty, and tough as old boots. She was surrounded by several tiny terriers that looked to Ronnie like a flock of agitated lavatory brushes. They barked continuously. 'You found your way,' she said, wading through them. Ronnie concentrated on not treading on one of them. 'Would you like to see the amenities first? This is the TV lounge.' She opened a door on a depressing room filled with old settees and armchairs. In one corner was a twenty-year-old TV set. 'We keep this for the evenings. This is where they come after dinner at five.'

'At five?' Ronnie said surprised.

'So they can watch the kiddies' programmes. Three good meals a day. Mr Flower. Breakfast at eight. Luncheon . . .' She gave it the full syllabic sonority. '. . . Luncheon at twelve and dinner at five. Everything weighed out to the last ounce. Everything wholesome.' She showed him the dining-room. It smelled of old plastic tablecloths.

'They're in their rooms now.' She looked at her watch.

108

'They go for walkies soon. We exercise them every day. Then in the afternoon they groom themselves. Mr Jolliffe and I are very keen on grooming. Keeps them up to the mark.'

'He around?' Ronnie said.

'Oh no, never at this time of a Sunday morning. Mr Jolliffe likes a lie in. Shall we go into the office?'

Ronnie sat on a hard chair surrounded by piles of old newspapers while Mrs Jolliffe squeezed behind an untidy desk. Beneath the acrid smell of old cigar-smoke he could detect another, which he might have described as a country smell. It was in reality the smell of ten thousand dogs overlaid by human old age.

'You got the papers?' she said. He fumbled in his briefcase. 'She sign happily enough?'

'Very happily,' Ronnie said, looking at the documents his mother had signed the last time they had worked on the VAT.

'That's good. We like our guests – we call them guests, you know – we like our guests to be happy here.'

'You're a bit cut off.'

'All to the good. We can't have old people wandering around towns, can we?'

'I suppose not.' He cleared his throat. 'What about the telephone?'

'Of course we *have* got a telephone. But we don't encourage our guests to use it. Naturally, if there was a crisis, Mr Jolliffe or I would ring you.' Her big square hands were ingrained by years of working at unpleasant jobs in cold weather.

'What about letters?' he said.

'They can write as many as they like. Why not? Of course, we look them over before sending them off. Don't want anyone distressed, do we?'

'I'll be living in Spain,' he said.

'Really?'

109

'Torremolinos.'

'Lovely. Mr Jolliffe and I have always wanted to go there. But when you're looking after people – Mr Jolliffe calls it a service, he says we are serving our community – well, when you're looking after people, you can't just go off for a holiday in Torremolinos.'

'It's permanent,' Ronnie said.

'How I envy you. What a life! And I don't want you to worry. Not one little bit. Your mum is going to take to this like a dog to a bone.'

'I hope so,' Ronnie said.

She smiled, showing stained teeth. 'You just wait and see.'

Maggie woke in the dim winter dawn, feeling Bill's big form in bed beside her. Going to bed with a man was nothing to waking up with him, she thought. If you loved him. And she did and she knew it and she was afraid of it. Take what you can while you can, she said to herself. Enjoy the now.

He slept on his side, knees drawn up, breathing surprisingly lightly for a big man. There was a delicacy about him which his size seemed to belie and which fascinated her. His gestures, his walk, the softness of his voice were all at odds with massiveness. The day before he had asked if he could sketch her and she had been amazed at the portrait's lightness of line and tone.

She got out of bed and went into the kitchen to make coffee.

As she waited for it to filter she thought how nice it would be not to have to go to work but to spend the day with him. But doctors were debarred from erratic behaviour.

She had always wanted to be a doctor, as her father had been and his father before him. There had always been doctors in her family. Before she married Alec she had practised briefly in another part of London, hadn't liked it and was only too pleased to come back to Pimlico. There were times when the work kept them apart and she had doubts about them both working, but after his death she had thanked God for the fact that work gave her little time to brood.

When the coffee was ready, she took a cup to Bill.

'Aah, that's good,' he said. 'Coffee hardly ever tastes as good as it smells. This does. What is it?'

'Java.'

' "I love the Java jive . . . " '

' "And it loves me," ' she added.

'What will your day be like?' he said.

'Hectic. It always is on Monday.'

'Dinner?'

'Of course. We'll have it here.'

'I have to pick up my father's things at the hospital, and I'm going to Greeley's. They were shut by the time I got there the other day.'

She finished her coffee. 'I must get going.'

'Wait.' He put his cup down. 'Don't go just yet.'

'Bill, I'll be . . .'

'Does it matter if you're five or ten minutes late?'

In the event, she was nearly fifteen minutes late and the waiting-room was full. Mrs Castle looked reproachful, but Maggie gave her no time to comment. She went straight through to her surgery.

For the next two hours she was absorbed with her patients, then there was a break. Mrs Castle brought her a cup of coffee and she sat sipping it, using the few minutes to relax. *I love the Java jive . . .* The phrase had remained in her mind. She could not even remember where she had heard the song.

Suddenly the name was there, pinched out of her sub-conscious. She picked up her telephone and dialled Bill on the top floor.

111

'I was just leaving,' he said.

'I've remembered that boy's name. Jarvis. Jack Jarvis.' The picture of his dying mother was clear. 'He lived in Jamaica.'

'Jamaica?'

'It's the name of one of the tower blocks around here. Tobago. Trinidad. Jamaica. Council flats. I'm going to see a patient there this morning. Why don't I pick you up at Greeley's in an hour, and you can have a look around if you want to?'

'Okay. See you there.'

Greeley's, the jewellers, was near Victoria Station. The windows were heavily barred. A sign stated, 'Sworn appraisers and valuers. We buy old gold and silver.'

Bill Seago studied the front of the shop, then went inside. It was old fashioned, with a mahogany counter and glass-fronted wooden display trays. An elderly woman with severely cut grey hair and a tweed suit was writing in a leather-bound ledger.

She looked over the top of her spectacles. 'May I help you?'

He caught the wary look he had seen before in the eyes of jewellers and he wondered if they half expected, some time during their lives, to look into the barrel of a pistol.

'I hope so,' he said. 'An old man brought something in to show you a few weeks ago. I think it was for a valuation. I want to find out about it.'

She smiled, showing her teeth like a horse. 'I'm afraid we don't give out information about our customers.'

He brought out a sheet of paper from his pocket. 'This is the letter you wrote to him.'

She glanced at it briefly. 'That's certainly our letter, but it doesn't change anything.'

'All I want to know is what it was he brought in. I'm his son. He died recently.'

'I'm sorry. But you can see our position.'

'Look, I came over from Boston to see him, and buried him instead. I have to list his belongings for probate. Now I can either get a court official to come and see you or you can tell me what it was so I know what I'm looking for. Do you remember him?'

'Yes I do. He was extremely rude! He brought in the brooch and wanted us to value it there and then. That's not how we do things.'

'I'm sorry he was rude to you. But I have to collect his clothes from the hospital this afternoon. I thought it might have been a ring, something small he could hide. But you say it was a brooch.' He could see that she regretted that. 'Can you tell me a little more about it? If you're in any doubt about me, you can call the Gerald Road Police Station. They know about it.'

The word 'police' seemed to have an effect. A look of irritation crossed her face.

'Mr Munday knows about it,' she said.

'Can I speak to him?'

'I'm afraid you can't.' There was a note of triumph in her voice. 'He's in Brighton, at the Trade Fair.'

'When will he be back?'

'Tomorrow.'

'I'll call him then.'

Maggie was double-parked outside the shop and he told her what had happened as she drove through the warren of streets of Pimlico, making for the huge complex of council flats by the river.

She stopped the car. 'Not a very nice sight, is it?' she said. They were looking at a concrete wasteland. There were apartment blocks as far as they could see, all six storeys high, built on stilts, with walkways and playing areas beneath and around them. They had been put up in the early sixties and must then have looked like the dynamic face of Britain; now they told a different story. The roadways seemed to be the last resting place of dead cars, some like amputees, without wheels. The swings, the see-saws and the roundabouts of the play area were smashed and derelict. The concrete had turned from light silver to a dark, stained grey with patches of white where the lime had emerged like a livid mould, and everywhere aerosol graffiti.

'This is where Jack Jarvis used to live,' she said.

'I think I'd sniff glue if I lived here.'

'I have to go to Number Sixteen. I'll probably be ten or fifteen minutes.'

'Okay. I'll walk through to the river.'

'He probably isn't here.'

'I'd like to know. Just to keep tabs on him.'

She took her bag and went across the exhausted grass. The lifts were out of order and she walked up the stairs to the first floor. She was uneasy, but told herself nothing could happen in broad daylight. She emerged into a long corridor. Everything was quiet, the place was deserted. She knocked at Number Sixteen. A young black woman opened the door.

'How's your mother?'

'About the same, Doctor.'

The flat smelled of eucalyptus and the fumes from a kerosene heater. It was a one-bedroomed flat. Maggie had visited it several times.

'Hello, Mrs Pocket.' As she greeted her, she could hear the wheezing in Mrs Pocket's chest. 'How are you today?'

'Not too bad, Doctor, not too bad.'

Mrs Pocket had chronic bronchitis and spent several weeks in bed each winter. Maggie took her temperature and listened to her chest. She knew there wasn't much she could do about Mrs Pocket. She was a school cleaner and started work at five in the morning come rain, come shine. She was also allergic to dust. But as she had said, 'What can a person do? You gotta earn your bread.'

Maggie talked for a moment, trying to cheer her up, then said, 'Do you know if a boy called Jack Jarvis lives here now? His mother was a patient of mine.'

Mrs Pocket shook her head. 'We keeps to ourselves. We don't know nobody.'

Maggie returned to the car. Bill had not returned yet and she entered the details of her visit on Mrs Pocket's card. When she had finished she looked about her but there wasn't a living soul to be seen. The mist was thicker here because of the river's proximity. It seemed to deaden the sound of traffic just as it did in Sebastopol Square. An old man came into view, pulling a shopping trolley. He crossed from left to right, then disappeared beneath one of the buildings. His fleeting presence made the place seem even bleaker. She sat for ten minutes, getting colder. It was more than half an hour since she had left the car for her visit. She wondered if Bill had got lost, for these apartments occupied about half a mile of the north bank of the Thames. The blocks were not built in a geometrically straight line but at angles to each other so that it was possible to be surrounded by concrete buildings and to become disorientated.

She left the car and walked along the pathway Bill had taken until she was cut off from the street and in the midst of concrete angles. She had not felt the wind so much at the car but now it came off the river and seemed to increase in velocity as it whipped through parking areas, under dark arcades and along the endless corridors. She stopped by what had once been a sandpit where children were meant to play and was now a small scummy pool. She could not imagine where he had got to. She struck off to her right. There was a series of narrow concrete alleyways linking one precinct with another. If he had gone down there he was walking parallel with the river and would never find the car. She hurried down one of the alleys.

Here the concrete walls were stained with blue and yellow paint. She was shivering with cold but also with a clammy dread. She hated this place and hated the thought that people like Mrs Pocket had to live in it.

In the dim light she saw that someone had discarded an old mattress in the alleyway. But as she came closer, it moved. It seemed to come slowly towards her. She stopped. It was making a kind of coughing noise. Then she recognised the mackintosh and ran forward. Bill was crawling on his hands and knees. He was barely conscious and blood was dripping from his nose and being blown from his mouth.

13

'Denise? Hello? Denise?'

'Who's this?'

'Hubert. Hubert Ringham. Can you hear me?'

The background was a confused mass of sounds: voices, hairdriers blowing, electric clippers buzzing. A voice shouted, 'Jacqui, will you check Mrs . . .'

'I waited for you all last evening,' Mr Ringham said.

'Yeah. Sorry about that.'

'I waited in the cold.'

'I was out. Down the country.'

'You? In the country? By yourself?'

There was a brief pause. 'Yeah. Went to see my mum.'

'You never told me you had a mum.'

'Everybody's got a mum. Stands to reason. She's in a home near Leatherhead. Called the "Byde-a-Wee".'

'But you never mentioned her before.'

'You never asked.' In the background a man's voice shouted her name. 'Look, I gotta go.'

'See you tonight then.'

'Not tonight.'

'Why not?'

'I said not tonight.'

The background voice called again, this time with irritation.

'When then?'

'I dunno. Maybe Sunday.'

'Denise, what's wrong?'

'Look, I gotta go.'

She rang off. Mr Ringham replaced the phone carefully, as though it was some fragile artefact. He sat back. Her mum? In a home? Denise?

Bill lay on the big double bed in Maggie's flat while she worked on his face. 'As far as I can tell, there's nothing broken,' she said. 'But I think you should have an X-ray.'

'I'll pass on that. I don't think there's anything broken either.'

'Your nose is going to be sore for a few days. Can you breathe yet?'

'A bit.' He pushed himself from the bed and stood up. She held his arm.

'How do you feel?'

'Less than Superman.'

She had taken away his shirt and sweater, which were covered in blood, and had brought down clean clothes. She helped him to put them on. 'I'll make you a cup of tea.'

'I know doctors don't recommend it at times like this, but I'd rather have whisky.'

She poured him a small drink and he sat down on the sofa in his usual place.

'How d'you think they knew?' she said.

'I don't think they did. I think they saw me. Maybe when I got out of the car.'

'How many were there?'

'It felt like a dozen. At the end of the alley there's a staircase leading up onto a different level. That's where they were waiting. You come out of the light into gloom and for a moment it's hard to see anything.'

'And you don't know what they hit you with?'

'It wasn't iron, thank God. That would have split my head open. Piece of two-by-four, probably. Something like that. It wasn't so much the blow, but the fall down the stairs.'

'I'm going to ring the police,' she said.

'What for?'

'What do you think?'

'What are you going to tell them?'

'Exactly what you've told me.'

'Look, you see a group of kids sniffing glue in the square. They frighten you. I step in. They don't like it. Later I get beaten up. I'm pretty sure they were the same kids, but I can't swear to it. There's nothing for the police.'

She sat next to him. 'Bill, I want you to stop what you're doing.'

'Why?'

'Because I don't think there's any real substance in what you suspect and I don't want you to get hurt again.'

He covered her hand with his own. 'Maggie . . .'

But she stood up and went to the window, staring out into the street as she spoke. 'I can't pretend I didn't know what was happening. I was afraid of it though.'

'These kids . . .'

'I'm not talking about them. I'm talking about me. And us.'

'Oh?'

'Just oh? I think I'm in love with you. No, I don't think, I know.' She held up a hand. 'Don't say anything, this is difficult enough anyway. You're going to say it can't work and that sooner or later, one way or another, you're going to go back to your life and leave me to mine. I know all that. I've thought about it and I've made my decision and when the time comes I'll live with it. But . . . I don't want you hurt again. I don't want anything happening to you. I don't want to have to wipe the blood from you again.'

119

For a second she saw Alec's smashed face and felt a tremor of horror.

He crossed the room and held her. 'I'll be careful,' he said.

She moved restlessly away and said, 'You know what I'd like best? To do what you wanted to do when you first came here. Get a couple of bikes and cycle down France. I'd like us to ride down to the Vaucluse and sit in the early spring sunshine in Arles and drink a bottle of wine.'

'There's always a but,' he said.

'Yes, there's always a but.'

Mr Ringham sat in his office with four bottles of dark Guinness stout on the desk in front of him. He had drunk three and was now on the fourth. He always drank Guinness when he was thinking. It stimulated the brain. He liked to believe it was a healthy drink. His thoughts, centred on Denise, had spread outwards like ripples.

'Mum!' he said out loud. 'What does she take me for?'

A single call to the 'Byde-a-Wee' retirement home near Leatherhead in Surrey had established that Denise did not have a mother there, nor a cousin nor an aunt nor any relative living or dead. Mr Ringham was a naturally suspicious man. She had lied to him. Why? Because she'd been out with another man, that's why.

So far, Mr Ringham's relationship with Denise had not precluded her seeing other men. He had not laid claim to her undivided attentions. He had assumed that a woman like her, generous in mind and body, would play the cards as they fell.

So why had she lied?

Why? Because she had not wanted him to know where she had been and that was bad, because it meant it had been important to her.

It was when he realised this profound truth that another, equally profound, presented itself to him. He considered his cold and miserable flat, considered spending his declining years there, collecting rents, scratching a living, alone most of the time.

He wasn't built to be poor, he wasn't built for solitude and discomfort. What he wanted was love and affection and flesh. He wanted a comfortable chair and a warm fire, three good meals a day, and a bottle of brandy when he fancied it. He wanted Denise.

He finished the last bottle of Guinness, took the empties back to the off-licence and bought four more. He looked at his watch. It was five o'clock. He didn't know how long hairdressers worked, but he imagined they had union hours like everyone else. She'd be finishing up at half-past probably. Half an hour to get home. Well, say three-quarters. Then he'd pay a little call. But in the meantime he remembered his own responsibility towards her and thought again of Numbers Twelve and Fourteen Sebastopol Square. In truth, he had recently thought of little else.

The file lay on his desk. Here were all the names of the tenants whose rents he had once collected. Miss Oppenheimer. Miss Krause. He noted that Mr Nedza's name was still there and he put a line through it as he had through the others. Only Mrs Mendel's remained active.

On the cover of the file was the name of the company which owned the houses, Fernlea Properties, with its address in the Vauxhall Bridge Road, to which he sent the cheque every month. Now it hardly seemed worthwhile. Even his own cut was not worth bothering about.

At half-past six he locked up his office and walked unsteadily into the Pimlico night.

When he reached Denise's flat he rang the bell and placed his ear near the door phone. He had already decided to say "Insurance inspection" when she said 'Who's there?', but in the event her voice said, 'You're early,' the lock buzzed and the door opened. He went

121

up the stairs. The door was ajar. He opened it, went into the room and closed it behind him. She was wearing her kimono and sitting on the side of her pink shiny bed, facing away from him, painting her fingernails. The very sight of her – or more precisely, the sight of those parts of her that were visible either plainly or through the thin fabric of the kimono – inflamed Mr Ringham's senses.

'I thought we said . . .' She turned. 'It's *you*!'

'Yes, it's me.'

'I said not tonight.'

'I know what you said. You said a lot of things this afternoon.'

She put down the nail varnish and waved her hands in the air.

'Mum!' he said, witheringly. 'I thought that was fishy. You never once mentioned a mum. And they never heard of your mum at that place near Leatherhead.'

'How do you . . .?'

'Because I phoned, that's how.'

'You got no right!' She was angry and rose to face him.

He had an urge to grasp her plump buttocks in his hands, but restrained himself.

'You lied to me.' His voice deepened with emotion. 'You were out with someone else.'

'Why shouldn't I? You don't own me.'

'Listen, Denise . . .'

'No, you listen. Who I go out with is my business. I admit we've had a bit of fun and all that, but it's over now.'

'Over!'

'I'm getting married.'

'What!' Mr Ringham was aghast.

'And I don't hold with married people playing around,' she said sententiously. 'It's sacred.'

He could hardly get his breath. 'Married!'

'Yeah. Married.'

'I don't believe it.'

'Don't you think I'm good enough? Don't you think anybody would have me?'

'It's not that. But I thought . . . I wanted to . . .' Mr Ringham fumbled for words and saw a look of irritation and contempt cross her face. He pulled himself together. 'Who's the lucky spouse to be?'

'The what?'

'Husband. The man.' Her eyes shifted away from him. 'You're not ashamed of him, are you?'

'No, I'm not. If you must know, it's Ronald Flower.'

'Ronnie Flower!' He burst out laughing and at the same time felt insulted that he should be rejected for that rotten twerp.

'There's no cause for you to take that attitude,' she said. 'He's been very good to me. And he's going to take me away from all this.' She swung her newly painted hand to encompass not so much the room, or even Pimlico, but the whole of South London and the hairdresser's shop in particular. 'We're going to live in Torremolinos.'

That was a severe blow to Mr Ringham. He could offer her nothing like Torremolinos. 'What, you, Ronnie and the old battle-axe? The three of you?'

'No, not the three of us. Just Ronnie and me. We're going to get a split-level house and a swimming pool.'

'And his mother?'

'None of your business,' she said. 'Now I want you out.'

'Listen, Denise, I . . .'

'Out! Out!' She advanced on him. He stepped back and found himself suddenly in the hall with the door closed. He opened his mouth to shout arguments, then realised how undignified that would be. He turned away and went down into the street. He thought of waiting for Ronnie, for it was clear he was the expected one. But that would be undignified, too. The best thing he could do was use his head. He decided to pick up a couple more bottles of Guinness.

'For me?' Mrs Mendel said.

'For you.' Bill held out a cardboard box of groceries.

'Why?'

'Because I want to,' he said.

'I can buy my own.'

'Of course you can. Look, there's birdseed. They told me at the shop they hadn't seen you for several days.'

'I don't only shop there,' she lied.

'Have you got a name for him yet?' She shook her head. 'But you'll keep him?'

'*Ja.*' The budgie flapped and fluttered in the cage. 'Would you like a cup of tea?'

He put the groceries in the kitchen. 'No thanks, not now. When were you last out of the flat?'

'I don't know. I can't remember.'

'Yesterday? The day before? When?'

She shrugged, not wanting to discuss it. Not going out had become important to her, like not hearing the telephone ring. It had become so bad her heart had nearly stopped every time until she had taken it off the hook and buried it under cushions.

'I went to the jewellers,' he said. 'It was a brooch.'

'So!'

'I think it must have been left to him. He was living with a woman in Guildford until she died.'

'Diamonds?'

'I don't know. The valuer wasn't there.'

'That was the money for the country! A valuable brooch he could sell. I thought it was his rubbish. But they ain't got it?'

'It's as it says in the letter. He wouldn't wait.'

She raised her eyes to the ceiling. 'You think?'

'It's possible. Of course, he might have put it in a bank.'

'He hated banks. Since I knew him he never went to banks.'

'Or asked a friend to keep it.'

'What friend? There is only me left.'

'I'm going to look around upstairs. His keys were with his clothes.'

'You can use my staircase.'

He went up onto the first floor to his father's flat and searched for nearly two hours. The first thing he did was move the wardrobe to see if there were any loose boards. There were not. He knocked the walls for hollow places that might have been papered over, pulled up the lino, looked beneath the carpets. He checked the linings of Stefan's clothing, the back of the old fireplace in case there was a loose brick or tile. He searched the three rooms as well as he knew how, but he found nothing.

'I'll leave his keys with you in case you want to go up for anything,' he said when he returned to Sophie's flat.

'I made some tea.'

The place depressed him, but he sat down.

'You like a biscuit?' she said.

'No thank you.'

'A big man like you!' He accepted a biscuit and dunked it in his tea. 'In Berlin before the war we always said the best biscuits came from England. And cloth for men's suits. Woollen goods.'

Caught by memory, she began to talk. As he sipped the tea she told him about her husband, Leo, and about Leni and the struggle to bring her up in the war and how she had died of pneumonia. She did not tell him about the young boys.

She went to the mantelpiece and brought back a photograph. 'That's Leni,' she said.

He looked at the picture and felt a stirring of cold inside him. Someone had coloured out one of her teeth and given her a moustache and drawn heavy breasts and pubic hair on the slim young body.

'Isn't she beautiful?' Sophie said.

'Yes,' he said. 'Very beautiful.'

Joan Deacon was twelve years old and went to a private school in Fulham. In winter, she left school between three and three-thirty, walked to the King's Road, caught a Number Eleven bus to the old BOAC air terminal and walked home from there. It was quite a long walk to her square and often she would drop into her father's office to give herself a break. She did so this particular afternoon.

Miss Marriner, the receptionist, looked up. 'Hello, Joanie.'

'Is my father in?'

Miss Marriner and Joan were not dissimilar, both on the plump side, both with problem skins. Miss Marriner was the older by a good ten years.

'He's on the phone,' she said. 'Did you watch *Midnight Express* last night?'

Joan shook her head. 'My father doesn't like me watching movies like that.'

Miss Marriner gave an elaborate shiver. 'Terrible, the things they did to that boy.'

Joan went into her father's office. He was talking on the telephone about property, which was what he always talked about. He smiled and waved a hand. On a table near the window there was a pile of magazines, among them several copies of *Country Life*, to which Deacon subscribed because they contained some of the best properties in Britain. Joan liked to look at the houses. She had her favourites, ranging from white terraces in Kensington and red-brick houses in Hampstead to the country mansions that had what were called 'stable blocks'. She couldn't make up her mind which she would have: probably both.

A house in the country and a house in town and either a Mercedes sports car or an open-top Beetle.

'Hi,' her father said, putting down the receiver. 'Have a good day?'

'All right.' She turned a page.

'What did you do?'

'Nothing much.'

'Homework all right?'

'We had a test in English. I got an A.'

'And you call that nothing! I call that terrific.'

Sometimes she was embarrassed by his enthusiasm. She turned over more pages and came to the society column: pictures of hunt balls; everybody holding glasses in their hands and smiling through their teeth. She hadn't decided whether she would take up hunting in the country. She thought perhaps not. Horses frightened her.

Her father picked up the phone again and was about to ask Miss Marriner to make a call for him when Joan said, 'A man spoke to me on the bus today.'

Kenneth's face froze. 'I told you never to talk to strangers.'

'I didn't talk to him, he talked to me. Anyway, he wasn't that sort of man.'

'How do you know what sort of man that is?'

'I know.'

'Go on.'

'He was just an ordinary man. He wore a black hat.'

'What did he want with you?'

'He knew me. He said he'd often seen me. Then he said he'd known grandpa.'

Kenneth picked up a pencil and tapped his teeth. 'Go on,' he said again.

'I thought grandpa went to Australia.'

'He did.'

'And he died there?'

'Yes.'

'This man thought he died here, in London. He said he'd tell me about it if there was more time.'

'I don't want you talking to people on buses. Anyway, he made a mistake.'

'He said he knew you, too. And he knew you were an estate agent.'

Kenneth sat in silence for a moment, then said, 'I think I'll pick you up at school for the next few days.'

'I mean, *why*?' Maggie said. 'Who'd do a thing like that?'

'Same person who'd put a rat in a birdcage,' Bill said.

They were in her surgery. He was sitting at her desk, working at the photograph of Leni with a soft rubber. He blew away the dust and held it close under the desk light. 'That's the best I can do.' The pencil marks had gone, but the slight indentations remained.

'Thank God her eyes aren't good enough to see it,' Maggie said.

'There isn't a light near the mantelpiece either.'

'Leni must have been a lovely girl.'

'I told her you'd think so, and that was why I wanted to borrow it, to show you.'

'She didn't mind?'

'It's difficult to tell whether she really minds something or not. It's all part of this image she produced of herself as a feisty old independent. I wonder if she's like that underneath?'

'I hope so. It'll give her strength. It's all she's got now. Otherwise she's alone.'

'Not completely.'

'How do you mean?'

'There's our friend who likes to draw on photographs. To put rats in cages.'

She began to pace restlessly. 'I wish she'd get out of that place.'

'I'd say that's what someone else wants too.'

She stopped. 'Rachmanism?'

'What?'

'There was a man called Rachman in London about twenty years ago. He bought up property with sitting tenants and then frightened them or used strong-arm tactics to get them out. His name went into the language.'

'She's sitting on a goldmine.'

Maggie nodded. 'Those two houses, empty, would be perfect for lateral conversion into luxury flats. The rest of the Square's already being redeveloped. I know she's been offered money to move.'

'By whom?'

'She didn't tell me. All the tenants were not so long ago. But where else could they go for the kind of rents they pay? And old people don't like to move.'

'I'll take this back to her tomorrow.' He put the photograph into an envelope. 'And I'll get someone to change her locks.'

'I tried to phone her today, but there was no answer,' Maggie said. 'She must have been out.'

'She hasn't been out for days. She's buried the phone under a pile of cushions. It's as though she wants to cut herself off from the outside world.'

'Five hundred and one . . . five hundred and two . . . five hundred and three . . .' Mr Ringham glanced at the slip of paper in his hand. 'Fernlea Properties. Five-o-three Vauxhall Bridge Road.' He looked at 503. It was a plain, three-storey office building about the size of a London house. It looked as though it had been built in the fifties. The red bricks were covered in soot and grime. The windows were devoid of curtains and blinds but had been coated on the inside with an impenetrable white paint.

On the door there had once been three or four name plates, but they had gone, leaving small rectangles and screw holes. The place appeared to have been empty for months.

He looked again at his piece of paper. No doubt at all. This was the address to which he had sent the rent cheques for the past year or more. He opened the letter-flap and was able to make out an uncarpeted passageway inside. Three or four envelopes lay on the floor.

It was nearly lunchtime and he was hungry, but he decided to wait. He crossed the road and took up a position on the far side from where he could watch No 503. Sooner or later someone would have to come and collect those letters.

Lunchtime came and went, and so did the early afternoon. Mr Ringham became extremely cold, but warmed himself by thoughts of what he might find out, and when he tired of those he allowed his mind to dwell on Denise. You had to have a goal in life, he thought, and Denise was his.

There was a café not too far away and at about three o'clock he bought himself coffee and a Danish pastry and stood near the window where he could keep the building in view. He made the coffee last as long as he could, but eventually he had to go back into the cold street. He paced up and down, trying to keep warm. It was nearly four o'clock when his patience was rewarded.

A woman went up to the door, took out a key and opened it. She bent down, retrieved the mail from the floor, closed the door and walked in the direction of Victoria Station.

He had been too far away to get a clear look at her face but there was something about the shape of it, of her body and her hair . . . something that pricked at his memory.

He had seen her before. Not too long ago. But where?

14

'So,' Mrs Mendel said to the budgie. 'And so. And again so.'

The bird hopped up and down, making sudden swipes with its beak at the cuttlefish stuck in the bars.

Her flat had been transformed. On every windowsill, in front of the door, on the steps of the back passage that led up into the house, in the bathroom above the bath, where the small window was cut into the wall, in the kitchen, below the kitchen window – in all these places she had set out her belongings: tins, cups, saucers, pots, pans, graters, strainers, china vases, old lampstands, brass candlesticks, potted plants or pots that had once held plants, ladles, empty bottles, casserole dishes, containers that had once held rice and flour, a spice rack, an old toaster, cake tins. Where there was no room on the interior windowsills, objects were placed near the doors so that the flat resembled a dim, subterranean junk shop where all the goods were on display.

'And here's another,' she said, putting a round paperweight she and Morris had bought in Devon on the floor near the door. 'If they come in this way, maybe an ankle, *ja?*' She thought of one of *them* tramping on the piece of solid glass, turning a foot, breaking a leg.

She paused and stood in one of the alleyways she had created between her furniture and looked about her. 'No more,' she said to the budgie. 'Enough.' She imagined someone entering while she slept, the noise of crashing china and banging tins. 'Like a minefield,' she said. 'Ain't it?' She looked about her. She was the only person who could confidently navigate the corridors remaining on the carpet.

Sometimes she felt so depressed that she wanted to make an end of it, but at others, like now, she felt better knowing she was *doing* something. When she was fighting back, even only hazily in her own head, she felt a sense of euphoria. Old muscles seemed charged with adrenalin born of aggression.

She had pulled out the plugs of all the lights in the house, removed the electric light bulbs from the ceiling fittings. Now only one lamp had a bulb in it, the table-lamp, which she could switch off in an instant. It had a line-switch hanging down below the table; no one could find the switch easily.

She turned off the light and plunged the flat into complete darkness. Slowly she moved along the pathways she had created. Only once or twice did her feet touch an object, and then so softly that it did not fall and make a noise.

She moved confidently towards the glass-fronted cabinet where Morris's china had been kept – it, too, was now doing sentry duty. In the dark her hand reached out to the small drawer on the right. She opened it noiselessly and drew from it a carbon-steel kitchen knife with a sharply pointed blade. It was about eight inches long, the same kind of knife she had used against the boy in Berlin so long ago. She stood at the sideboard, quite still, for some seconds, then she put back the knife, and switched on the light. She was pleased with what she had achieved.

Perhaps it was the sudden noise or the sudden light which made the budgie panic. It began to flutter and flap in its cage, flying against the thin metal bars. All the while it made frightened noises in its throat.

Sophie watched it for a moment. The bird landed in the centre of the cage and looked about desperately for a way out.

'*Ja, liebchen*,' she said. 'You have your cage. I have mine.'

'Well, you're not as beautiful as you were,' Maggie said, inspecting Bill's nose and the dark bruising on the left side which covered his cheekbone. 'But you'll do.'

'It's in the eye of the beholder,' he said.

It was mid-afternoon and the light was fading fast. She had gone up to his apartment to examine his injuries.

Their relationship had deepened. Their passion had increased with familiarity. She knew she was sliding deeper and deeper into a morass from which it would be difficult to climb out, and sometimes she was gripped by nervous tension amounting almost to hysteria as she thought of the inevitable outcome.

'What do you feel like tonight?' she said.

He smiled that melon-shaped face-cracking smile that she found so infectious. She moved hastily away and said, 'In the way of food, I mean.'

He did not eat hugely, as she had expected for a man of his size, but he knew about food and appreciated it. Now he tapped his stomach and said, 'I've put on five pounds in a week. What about a steak and salad.' He took a ten-pound note from his wallet.

'Don't be silly. You know I . . .'

'We treat our women roughly in Boston,' he said. 'You want me to stuff it down your bra?'

She backed away smiling. 'I'll take it!'

'Where are you going now?'

'To the butcher's near Victoria.'

'I'll ride with you as far as Greeley's, then I'll walk back and take Leni's picture to Mrs Mendel. I want to talk to her.'

She noticed his writing-block and notes covering several pages. Catching her glance, he said, 'I'm trying to put down everything I know, from the time they found his body on the steps.'

The thought struck her that the moment he became convinced his father had died in an accident he would make his plans to leave and she would lose him. They stared at each other and it seemed almost as though he knew what she was thinking; unspoken words hung in space between them. They never mentioned him leaving, never talked about the future.

They went downstairs and walked along the side of the square opposite to Mrs Mendel's house. Her little Renault was wedged between a battered panel van and the hulk of an old Citroën which had settled down on its axles like a dying shark.

Bill saw it first. He checked his stride, then caught her arm. 'Christ!' he said. 'The bastards!'

The silver-grey car looked as though it had been mugged. Paint-stripper had been thrown over the bonnet, leaving it streaked and raw. The aerial had been twisted and broken and there were deep scratches on the sides where someone had taken a sharp weapon and pulled it along the paint. She shivered, with a kind of horror that anyone should do this to her.

Bill walked around the car, inspecting it. He kicked the tyres. 'They're okay. When did you last use it?'

'Yesterday. I didn't have far to go on my rounds this morning, so I walked.'

'Probably happened last night then.'

The horror was replaced by anger. 'Who would do a thing like that? Who . . .?' She stopped. 'You don't think . . .?'

'Of course.'

'Those boys?'

'Who else?'

134

After a moment she said, 'This sort of thing happens quite often in London.'

'Don't kid yourself.'

'But why?'

'Good question. I can just understand why they came for me. But you . . .?'

'I wonder . . .' She told him about Jack Jarvis's mother, the young boy standing next to the bed filled with hate and grief and frustration.

'I thought there was some scheme, some plan to the violence,' he said slowly. 'But this doesn't fit. It's formless.'

She had been walking round the car, looking at the damage and feeling her anger grow.

'I'm going to the police,' she said.

'You want me to come with you?'

'No. It's my car.' She had not meant to say it so abruptly, but her anger was difficult to control.

He turned. 'See you later,' he said, and walked away.

'Where are you going? Bill!'

He didn't seem to hear and moved rapidly in the direction of Inkerman Street and the river.

All his life, Mr Ringham had been a collector. As a child he had bartered for marbles and stamps and cigarette-cards, later it had been beer mugs and Victorian knick-knacks. None had given him any real satisfaction and eventually they had bored him. He discovered that there were only two things he positively liked to collect and of which he never tired: the first was money and the second information. He had collected the former so sedulously that he'd had to spend some time in prison. But that was past. Now he was collecting information which, he was certain, would lead in the fullness of time to its conversion into coin of the realm.

He stood pondering this aspect of his character halfway up Raglan Street, opposite the old Orpheum Cinema,

135

which was now a bingo hall. The afternoon was drawing in, dusk was filling the streets and the air was freezing. He stamped his feet and pulled his coat more closely about him. He looked at his watch: they'd be out soon.

He had spent many happy hours in the Orpheum in his childhood. His mother would give him a bob or two on a Saturday morning and he'd be off like a bullet, especially if it was a Tom Mix or a William Boyd picture. He'd seen *Little Caesar* there, and *Scarface* and *The Ziegfeld Follies* and all those Hollywood pictures which showed lovely big houses on tree-lined streets and everybody well fed and well dressed and driving those big open cars. They had formed his desires. He'd had one chance and that had gone wrong. Now he was being given another. He wasn't sure where the smaller pieces of the jig-saw fitted. He had some, but not others. But Hubert Ringham had cut his teeth on jig-saws.

He heard a roaring noise coming from the hall and he knew it was the sound of chairs being pushed back. The bingo session was over. They started coming out, mainly pensioners, a few men, but mostly elderly women. A large figure came through the swing doors and began to descend the steps. 'Thought she'd be last,' he said to himself. What *did* she look like? He crossed the street and came up behind her. She was moving slowly and steadily. An elephant, he thought. That's what she looked like from the rear, an elephant's bum.

'Evening, Mavis,' he said, drawing up with her. 'You get lucky?' Everyone knew that Mrs Flower played bingo three afternoons a week.

Mavis Latter, he thought. Who'd believe it? She'd been quite pretty in the old days, in the Alma Street School. He'd fancied her himself. Then Sidney Flower (deceased) had stepped in. Now look at her.

'How's the fibrositis?' he said.

'Don't ask!'

136

'Business all right?'

She gave a non-committal grunt. They walked on in silence for a few moments, then he said, 'I hear you're going to the land of flamenco.'

'What?'

'Spain. That's what I heard. That you were going to live in Spain.'

'Me? Spain?'

'I thought there must be . . .'

'Ronald. That's who's going to Spain.'

'To live?'

'Course not. Holiday.'

'I could've sworn I heard . . .'

'Torremolinos.'

'Funny how rumours get about. Funny how things change when people tell them. I must have heard wrong.'

'We never had no holidays when we were young,' Mrs Flower said mordantly, rolling on down the pavement.

'That's true enough.'

'Spain. A fortnight. And what am I supposed to do? What happens if I get ill? What happens if there's . . . if there's a crisis?'

'What d'you mean, a crisis?'

'In the business. Taxes and that.'

'I suppose that's Ronnie's department. Must be good to have someone like him around the place. Sharp as a tack they said when he was a boy.' She sniffed. 'I mean, to deal with the paperwork. Remember at school?'

'What do you mean?'

'I sometimes think of that,' he said. 'They were so unfair to you.'

She looked at him under her eyelids. 'I don't know what you mean.'

'Come on, Mavis, you know exactly what I mean. They used to make you stand in a corner. I reckon you must have spent most of your school-days in a corner.'

137

She stopped and turned on him fiercely. 'That's not true!'

'What I'm trying to say is that it wasn't *your* fault. These days they've got a name for it. It's called dyslexia.'

'What?'

'Word blindness. Lots of kids have it. It's not their fault. They're born like that.'

'You having me on?'

'Scout's honour,' said Mr Ringham, who had never been a Scout.

They continued on down the street.

'What's it called?'

'Dyslexia. I mean, that's why you never did well, Mavis.' He remembered her vividly now, stumbling over words, incapable of reading. Their English master had described her as being as thick as two planks. For nearly a year that's what everyone had called her, 'Plank'.

'You'd have got special treatment today. You should've got it. Only in those days the word hadn't been invented.'

'They used to say I was . . .' she began indignantly.

'I know they did.' His tone was soothing. 'That's what I'm saying. Unfair. So it's good you've got Ronald.'

'Yes.' She was suddenly full of self-pity. 'He's a good boy. To tell you the truth, I don't know what I'd do without him. Close up the shop, I suppose. Get out. It's those forms. Forms, forms, forms. And I can't make them out. I mean this VAT. It's just beyond me.'

'It's beyond most of us. And Ronnie does all that?'

'All of it. I sign, and that's all I got to do.'

'You ought to thank your lucky stars for Ronnie,' Mr Ringham said. 'It won't be so easy once he's gone though. You'll have to make arrangements.'

'You mean on holiday?'

'No. I mean for good. Still, you can always get an

accountant. He'll sort things out – 'course, they cost the earth.'

'What d'you mean, for good?' She had stopped again, to face him, fear in her eyes.

'When he gets married. Stands to reason a bright chap like Ronnie'll be scooped up one day.'

'Oh, married.' He could see her relax with relief. 'Ronald's not getting married. Hasn't even got a girlfriend. Anyway, there's no one'll look after him as well as me.'

'Here's my street,' Mr Ringham said, and raised his Homburg.

He bought himself a couple of bottles of Guinness and went to his office, where he sat down at his desk. After an hour, when the bottles were empty, he knew he had more of the jig-saw in his head. In fact, if he laid it out piece by piece, it formed quite a clear picture. He picked up his phone and dialled.

When Ronnie Flower answered, he said, 'Good evening, Ronald.' He had never called him Ronald before and the use of it now carried mysterious undertones. 'I wondered if I could have a word with you.'

'Okay.' Ronnie's voice sounded surprised and wary. 'Except I've gotta go out in a minute. Got an appointment.'

That'll be Denise, Mr Ringham thought savagely. 'I don't mean on the phone.'

'Oh? What's it about then?'

'Property.'

'What about property?'

'I thought of going into the property business.'

There was silence at the other end, then. 'So why are you telling me?'

'You're a man of parts, Ronald. You've lived in the district all your life. I thought you were the chap I should speak to, get a bit of advice.'

'What do you mean, going into property, then?'

139

'You know, become a developer.'

'You want to become a developer?' Ronnie laughed.

'You find it amusing?'

'You up to something?'

'I don't think I like either the tone or the phrase.'

'Don't kid me. You got done. You been inside. I know that.'

'That's past. The debt's paid.'

'I gotta go. Nice talking to you.'

'I don't think you understand,' Mr Ringham said. 'Let me tell you my ambitions. I want . . .'

'Listen, Ringham, I've had it. You go and tell your ambitions to someone else.'

'A place in the sun, Ronald. That's what I want. We all want that. Some sunny country. Spain, perhaps.'

'Spain?'

'Yes. Spain. Funnily enough, I've just been talking to your mother. I met her on her way home from bingo. I was telling her that. The land of flamenco, I called it. Ever heard flamenco?'

'I don't know what this is all about, Ringham, but . . .'

'Used to be a very cheap country when the General was still alive. That's all finished now.'

'You been drinking?'

'As a matter of . . .'

'Either that, or you're senile.'

'Just so we're not in doubt about anything, so we know exactly what we're talking about, I'll draw you a picture. Just say . . .'

'For Christ's sake! I'm late and . . .'

'Humour me. Just say I knew where there was a shop in a small way of business. One of the old-fashioned kind. And next to that shop there were two empty houses. No, I'd be wrong if I said that. *Nearly* empty. That makes three houses in a row. What if I said this area was being developed and you could get planning permission to build a hotel there, or an office building, or just do up the houses and sell them. Just as houses they've got to be worth nearly a million.'

'Go on.'

'What if there was an old woman living in one and no one could get her out except by making her life so bloody miserable that she got out on her own?'

There was a pause, then Ronnie said, 'That's two houses. What about the shop?'

'Oh yes, the shop. What if the shopkeeper was the owner of the other houses? See? Then there'd be three? What if he'd already bought the houses when there's only old people in them, and then they begin to die, one after the other.'

'You make me laugh,' Ronnie said. 'You know that? You really make me laugh. You ring me up with some cock-and-bull story . . . you've gone barmy! You think anyone would believe what you're saying?'

'Yes, I do, Ronald. I know a lady of our mutual acquaintance who'd believe me, specially if I told her where she was going to spend her declining years. You see, she doesn't know, Ronald. It's going to be a surprise, apparently.'

Silence. Then a voice cold with hate said. 'Where?'

'Lovely place near Leatherhead,' Mr Ringham said. 'Now, shall we meet? Somewhere safe where we can talk in private.'

Ronnie needed time to think. 'All right,' he said abruptly. 'Only I gotta go now. I'll work out somewhere. Ring me back.'

'I will,' Mr Ringham said. 'You can be sure of that.'

When Maggie came up from evening surgery she heard Bill upstairs. The sounds were comforting and she thought of the silence that would greet her once he left and felt a spasm of depression. She dialled his flat.

'Hi, landlady.' His voice was warm and reassuring. The mood of the afternoon seemed to have gone.

'Is it time for a drink?' she said.

'I'll be down in a minute.'

She looked out into the dark night. It had been sleeting earlier, now this had turned to snow. He came down and she gave him a drink and he took his usual place on the sofa. He patted the empty cushion beside him and she said, 'Talk first.'

'All right. You went to the police?'

'It was a waste of time.'

'You had to go, though, You had to report something like that.'

'That's what they said. Thank you for reporting it.'

'That was all?'

'Oh, no, lots more. I was there for about an hour, but that's what it amounted to. According to them, this sort of thing happens every day. It's petty crime, and they're in business to deal with serious crimes.' Her voice was angry.

'You can see it from their point of view.'

'Don't you start! After the Brixton riots and the general hullabaloo they've had to draft men out of areas like Pimlico to the trouble spots, so crimes like car-bashing can't be properly investigated. The Inspector didn't put it quite that way, but that's what it amounts to. They took down everything I told them and typed it out and made me sign it and they're going to get in touch.'

'Did you mention the kids?'

'Yes.'

'And what happened in the Square?'

'No. I just said there was a group of boys around that I thought had been sniffing glue. They said they knew that. They said there were dozens of groups of kids sniffing glue – and a lot worse – and they didn't have the manpower to do anything about that, either. In fact, they gave me the impression it was more a Social Services job

142

than a police investigation. That was my afternoon. How was yours? You went looking for them, didn't you?'

He nodded. 'I walked all over that estate. Grim, isn't it?'

'It was only built twenty-five years ago. Now they're talking of pulling it down.'

'I never saw any boys, although the evidence is all there. I looked into hallways and areas behind the stairs, that sort of place. There were small plastic bags and empty tubes of solvent everywhere. Then I walked down to Greeley's. Hang on a second . . .'

He went upstairs and returned with a brooch in his hand. 'My father had taken it back to the shop.'

It was a curious piece of jewellery about six inches long, and narrow. It was made of roughly worked silver, inlaid with ivory and semi-precious stones.

She took it from him, and examined it. 'I've never seen anything quite like it.'

'The guy at the shop, Mr Munday, said he thought it came from Morocco. He'd seen one or two, but not for a long time. It's the kind of thing naval officers brought back to their wives or girl-friends in the twenties.'

'It's very heavy.'

'He said it wasn't worth much, so there's the end of my dreams of luxury. It would have been the end of my father's dreams of moving to the country, too. In a way, I'm glad he didn't live to be disappointed.'

She turned it over, looking at the long steel pin that formed the clip. 'What are you going to do with it?'

'Give it to Mrs Mendel.'

'That's a lovely idea. She can put it in her display cabinet. She might even have some place to wear it. It'll always remind her of your father.'

Kenneth Deacon stood at his office window looking out at the line of cars moving slowly up Belgrave Road towards Vauxhall Bridge. It was rush hour and light snow was falling. It looked like his idea of hell. He jingled the change in his pocket and began to pace up and down the room. He was restless and filled with explosive nervous tension. He knew what was wrong. He wanted Maggie. He not only wanted her in bed, but he wanted to see her decorating the far side of a restaurant table or the passenger seat of his new BMW. His mind went back over some of the evenings they had spent together. The times with her had been the high spot of his week. She wasn't only attractive, there was an air of quality about her, something Edna had never possessed. He would never have considered buying property on the Isle of Wight and joining the clubs – perhaps he might even try for one of the Cowes yacht clubs – with Edna. But Maggie was a different matter. There was something cool and reserved about her, as though she had created a wall around herself. He did not delude himself that he had broken down this wall yet, but it was something he had set himself to do. And he still might. He wasn't going to let a bumbling American interfere with his plans.

The irony was that it was he, Kenneth, who had sent Seago to Maggie. Well, he'd said he was only going to stay for a month or two. When he went, she would be lonelier than ever. And so far he had no actual proof that anything *was* going on between them.

He wondered if he should telephone her, just to keep her interested. He could tell her about Thursday. Tell her they'd go somewhere really classy like the Savoy Grill or the Connaught. See what the reaction was.

He dialled on his private line but her receptionist said she was still seeing patients and he left a message asking her to ring him back.

There was a knock on his door and Miss Marriner said. 'I've got Joan on the line. And, if there's nothing else, I'll get off home.'

He talked to his daughter for a few moments. There

was a concert at school that evening. She was just ringing to tell him she was going with someone's parents.

He put the receiver down, got up and began his restless pacing again. For the past few days he had taken Joan to school and picked her up, but he couldn't spend his life doing that. The man on the bus had to have been Ringham. What the hell was his game? Blackmail?

In the old days he had been fond enough of him, when Ringham had come to fetch him from school or had been detailed by his father to take him to a circus or a fair. Then there had been the shame of the arrests: God, that had been terrible! 'Trust Fund Scandal,' the papers had screamed. 'City Solicitor And Clerk Arrested For Fraud'. The humiliation had been so great that Kenneth had stayed indoors for weeks, refusing to go to school. He imagined that everyone in the streets, everyone sitting in the Underground or on a bus was looking at him and thinking, 'That's Kenneth Deacon. His father's gone to gaol.'

But that was a long time ago and the old man had died in Pentonville and everyone had forgotten. Kenneth had lived with an aunt and uncle in Southampton for the remainder of his schooling and young manhood, then he'd returned to Pimlico when he had met Edna and married her.

Now Ringham had surfaced like some unwelcome sea creature and had started his little games. Why all of a sudden? They had known each other's whereabouts, but by unspoken mutual desire they had kept out of each other's lives. Why had this changed?

He didn't want Joan disturbed. She didn't know about her grandfather's imprisonment and there was no need for her to know. He didn't want her suffering the shame he had suffered.

He phoned Maggie again, but the line was engaged. He locked up his safe and the filing cabinets and left the

145

office, locking the big outer door behind him. He was turning to walk towards Prince's Square when he heard his private phone ringing. He unlocked the door again. But it was secured by three locks and by the time he got inside the ringing had stopped. He was sure it had been Maggie. He dialled her number but again heard the engaged tone. He put the receiver down and waited in case she should ring again. Nothing happened. He decided to go home, change and drive round to see her. It was too easy on the phone for a woman to say she was tired or busy.

Sophie Mendel was dreaming about Berlin. She dreamed about the city more and more these days. Her dreams were always of the months just after the end of the war, when she and Leni had returned. It was a city of dust and rubble then; whole streets were gone. Many buildings that had survived were unsafe and had to be pulled down, so the days were punctuated by the roar of falling bricks and mortar. And this was her dream: she was standing in the street outside the cellar watching a church being demolished. First the steeple was brought down and then the walls and the dust billowed out and a great roaring noise echoed across that part of the city.

She awoke, sitting in her own flat in the 'Crimea' in front of her bubbling gasfire. The roaring was still in her ears, inside her head. She sat still. The bird flapped and fluttered in anxiety. Had there been a knocking? Had that formed the pattern for the dream?

'Is there someone?' she called.

There was no answer.

Cautiously she went to the door, and stood listening. 'Who is there?' But again there was only silence.

She raised the flap of her letter-box, shone the beam of her torch outside, and found herself looking at a pile of garbage. Someone had emptied a couple of bins into

146

the basement area in front of her door. This was the noise she had heard.

She could not imagine anything much worse. Cleanliness had been a touchstone all her life. Even when she and Leni only had a cellar, she stacked the rubble on either side of her entrance, so that she had a walkway into the street, as though she had dug a lane through a snowdrift. She had kept that lane swept and washed. With all the buildings being demolished, Berlin was a city of dust. The cellar had a concrete floor. Dust made dust. She had fought it with all her strength, trying to give Leni and herself somewhere clean to eat and sleep. She had always had a horror of other people's dirt.

She put on a pair of household gloves and brought an old coal scoop from the kitchen. The rubbish had fallen against her door and she had to struggle to open it. Among the vegetable matter, the tins and bottles she saw rotting meat and offal, fish carcases that were almost phosphorescent with decay. 'Horrible!' she said. 'Horrible, horrible!'

It took her nearly an hour to clean it away into her own dustbins. Then she washed the basement area and the steps with warm, soapy water. While she was working, something changed fundamentally in Sophie Mendel. Until then she had nursed a dichotomy. Part of her mind told her that the recurring phenomena that had been plaguing her were born of human agency; the other half had heard the house itself in its anguish and recalled the ectoplasmic speculations of Mr Ringham. This was the area of her mind which harked back to the dark Nordic past of runes and magic and fetches. Now she blotted it out.

'They want us out of this house!' she said to the budgie. 'But we shall not go.'

Iron had entered her soul and a cold anger fed her old muscles with energy. She looked about her flat with clearer vision. She had given herself a certain safety margin, but at the same time she had created a cage and a cage could be a trap. She thought of Winston, trapped in the cage by a rat. She was not going to let that happen to her.

Her strength, she thought, was knowledge. 'Who knows the house better than I?' she said to the bird. But she had to know what the house was hiding from her. Only an hour before the thought of finding out would have turned her bowels to water; now she picked up her powerful torch, found the bunch of keys which had once belonged to Stefan and been given to her by the American. Lastly, she took from the sideboard drawer her eight-inch kitchen knife. She went to the staircase that led from her kitchen and found herself in the still silence and freezing passages of the house.

She played the torch over the walls and decided to see what keys Stefan had kept all these years. If he'd had an affair with Lily, then maybe he had a key to her flat. He did. She opened the door. The room was empty, shuttered by corrugated iron, a drift of old newspaper pages on the floor and a smell of old fires. That was all. She went on up into Stefan's flat, but it was the same as when she had last seen it. There were still keys she had not used. She looked across the landing to the double doors joining the two houses. She tried each key in turn and at last heard the old lock tongue snap back. So Stefan had had more than one girl-friend. She pushed open one half of the double doors and played the torch through the opening. She found herself looking at a mirror image of the house in which she stood: the landing, then an apartment. This one, which had belonged to Eva and Carl, was open. It was where they had asphyxiated themselves. She could see into it. The windows were not boarded up and the street-lights outside had a quality of moonshine. She had been in here many times to take coffee with them.

She looked through the well remembered rooms which were now only walls, floors and ceilings. Even the heater which had killed them was gone.

She had come up from her own flat with all the energy produced by her anger, now this was beginning to drain away. Exhaustion was overtaking her, but she knew she must not give up now. She had to go through the other apartments and then down to the basement where once Miss Krause had lived. She must search the two houses, prove to herself either that there was nothing strange or, if there was, know that it had form and volume. She played the torch on the old stained wallpaper of the stairwell, gripping the wobbly handrail, hearing her feet on the bare wooden boards. Clack . . . clack . . . clack . . . clack. She stopped, listening. There had been, she thought, another sound. She concentrated, but heard nothing.

She moved on slowly down the stairs and began to smell an unfamiliar odour, something of petrol about it, and yet not quite. She stopped again, for again she thought she had heard something in the house above her. Were the timbers contracting? Had her own footsteps, her own fragile weight, shifted the balance on joists and beams so that a readjustment rippled through the old floorboards as the house accommodated her? She had to be firm with herself. This was the time when the mind flew into the night. 'Come, Sophie,' she said softly. 'Be a brave girl.'

Holding the knife in her right hand and the torch in her left, she went down a few more steps and the smell became stronger. It was coming from the apartment on the ground floor of the empty house. It had once been occupied by a Russian countess. At least, she had said she was a countess, but many Russians falsely claimed a title. Had she been Stefan's girlfriend, too?

The door was closed but not locked. The handle glinted, polished, in the light of the torch. She turned it, the smell overwhelmed her. She felt her senses reel. She

149

played her torch along the walls. An old bookcase, patches on the paper where pictures had been. Then on the floor – and here it was different. There were three mattresses and some pillows and stubbed-out cigarettes and dozens of small plastic freezer bags and, in the corners where they had been thrown, what looked like forty or fifty squeezed-out toothpaste tubes. She bent to pick one up and as she did so she heard a noise just outside the door: a scraping like a soft footstep on one of the bare treads. She switched off her torch and the room went black. She shrank back behind the door, holding the knife in front of her. The door was pushed gently open and she could feel the presence of another person.

The windows of this apartment were also covered in corrugated-iron but it had holes in it where bolts had once been used, and through these holes bars of light broke into the room. Each was blotted out in turn as someone moved across the floor in front of them.

A voice said softly, 'Mrs Mendel.'

She flicked on the torch and saw him in front of her. He grabbed at the knife, and she dropped it. She was looking up at Stefan's son.

'What are you doing here?' he said.

'What are *you* doing here?' Her fright turned to rage.

'I was coming to see you. I saw lights in the upstairs rooms. I didn't know it was you. I guess I thought someone was trying to frighten you. Then I saw the door in the passageway to your flat was open. That made me really worried.'

Her suspicion died slowly. 'What do you want with me?'

'I was bringing Leni's picture back, and a present from my father.'

'Look,' she said. 'People have been here.' She pointed the torch-beam at the floor. 'What is the smell?'

'Glue.'

150

'Glue? What glue? Why?'

'Let's go downstairs. I'll explain it to you and then we'll go to the police.'

She stiffened. 'The police? I won't . . .'

'Yes, you will, Mrs Mendel. And I'll come with you.'

15

'You want a finca-style or a split-level?' Denise said.

'What?'

They were in Denise's flat. She was lying on her stomach on her bed, dressed only in her kimono and turning the glossy pages of a house magazine.

'Finca-style, it says here, Spanish farmhouse style. Look.' She showed him a picture of a white-walled house built with small windows, a great deal of black wrought-iron work and terracotta tiles on the roof. 'Or a ranch-style, split level with a walled swimming pool and built-in barbecue. How does that sound?'

'Unh,' Ronnie said.

The kimono was tight over her buttocks and at any other time Ronnie might have nibbled her. Now his mind was on that old fart Ringham. He'd weasled and winkled and put things together and now he'd be wanting a piece of the action. Bloody old criminal.

'Why don't you say something?' Denise said. 'D'you like the farmhouse?'

'I dunno.'

'What about the ranch-style?'

'Yeah, they look great.'

'Which *one*, though?'

'For Christ's sake, we don't have to make up our minds right now!'

'You cross about something?'

'No. I got something on my mind, that's all.'

'Well, you better get it off. We got things to do. I mean, when do I give in my notice? What about the wedding? We got to book the registry office. We got to get licenses. You can't just put everything off until the last moment. We got to make preparations. You won't even tell me when the wedding day *is*. It's not fair. What about your mum, have you told her?'

Christ, Ronnie thought, what a question. That was the last thing he was going to do. And it was the last thing Ringham was going to do, if Ronnie had his way. That was the difficult part, his mum. He'd have to tell her they were taking her away . . . but where? He could always say one of them health spa places. That was an idea. Somewhere that specialised in backs and legs and heads and arms and livers and kidneys . . . She'd be bound to fall for that. But first of all he'd deal with Ringham.

'I got to choose a dress,' Denise said. 'You don't just go and get married in a pair of old jeans, you know.'

'Don't you?' Ronnie said.

'No, you don't.'

'Well, you'd know, wouldn't you.'

'What's that supposed to mean?'

'Only that you been married before.'

'You trying to pick a fight?'

''Course I'm not.'

'Cause if you are, I'll oblige.'

'Listen . . . Denise . . .' He put his hand on her bottom, but she took it away.

'None of that.'

'Oh, I don't know, there's no pleasing you sometimes!'

'You can please me easily enough by making up your mind.'

The telephone rang in her hall. She answered it and flounced back. 'It's for you! Who you been telling?'

He went to the phone, closing the door behind him. 'Yeah?' he said softly.

'Good evening, Ronald.' He was disguising his voice, but Ronnie recognised Ringham.

'How did you know I was here?'

'I know everything about you, Ronald.'

Ronnie felt his hands go cold.

'It's about the meeting,' Ringham said.

'I got an idea about that,' Ronnie said.

They talked for a few minutes, then he put down the receiver. Denise opened the door.

'Who was that?'

'I got to go.'

'Ronnie!'

But he went down the stairs and into the street. She slammed the door after him.

He walked to the telephone-box at the corner of Sebastopol Square, put in money, dialled a number, and waited. The phone rang and rang, but no one answered.

Maggie was in her flat when the bell rang. She picked up the door-phone. 'Bill?'

'Hello Margaret, it's Kenneth.'

For a moment she could say nothing. She was surprised and at the same time felt a twinge of guilt. She began to say that she was busy, that she was about to go out on her rounds, but found she couldn't.

She pressed the door-release. 'Come up.'

She looked hastily around the sitting-room to see if there was anything of Bill's left around and thought at the same time, What the hell does it matter? It's got nothing to do with him. But it *did* have something to do with Kenneth, there was no denying it.

She went out onto the landing to greet him. He

was wearing an expensive Missoni cardigan in shades of tan and green. He smiled and reached for her. She gave him her cheek and said, 'This is a surprise.' He smelled of aftershave.

In the sitting-room, she watched his eyes move quickly around. Was he seeking the same evidence she had looked for a moment earlier?

'You're looking very smart,' she said. 'New?' He was a good-looking man, there was no doubt about that.

'Yes.'

'It's lovely.'

'Thank you. You're looking very nice yourself.'

She gave a mock bow. The phrases hung in the air like washing.

'Drink?'

She gave him a vodka and tonic and took a Perrier for herself. 'I have to see patients,' she said before he could comment.

They talked weather and children and about his business and she found it difficult to concentrate for she knew that Bill would soon be home.

'I called you,' he said.

'I've been very busy.'

'I thought you must have been.'

'It's my worst time. Flu, bronchitis. Roll on the spring.'

'So I thought I'd chance it and come round.'

'I'm just sorry it's . . .' She looked at her watch.

'I know. You've got your rounds. No, I was passing, and I dropped in to see what you'd like to do on Thursday.'

He hadn't been passing, she thought. You didn't pass Balaclava Place unless you were going to the Square, and that wasn't Kenneth's scene. And you didn't put on a new Missoni cardigan unless you wanted to be noticed.

'Thursday?' she said.

'I thought we'd do something different. An early show

and then push the boat out a bit. I've got something cooking up that'll need celebrating.'

'I'm not sure . . .'

'The Savoy or the Connaught. You choose a place.'

She realised he had decided to ignore their last contact, to pretend that nothing had happened and that their lives were progressing steadily as usual.

'Kenneth, I . . .'

'Somewhere really special.'

The moment had gone. He seemed to take her acceptance for granted, for he changed the subject. 'How's your tenant getting on?'

'Mr Seago?'

'Yes, the American. Any idea when he's going?'

'No.'

'As far as I could gather it wasn't to be for long.'

'No.'

'You'll miss him. I mean the company, having someone else in the house.'

She could not meet his eyes. Did he know? Had he guessed? Certainly he had seen them together once, on a day she had refused to out with Kenneth. She remembered the anger in his eyes.

'Would you like me to start looking round for someone to replace him? We get half a dozen requests a day for furnished accommodation.'

He's probing, she thought, and suddenly she no longer cared. 'Kenneth, I don't think Thursday's a good idea.'

'Oh? Why not?'

'This is difficult for me. I'll try to explain how I feel. We met at a bad time for both of us. We'd lost the people we loved and our lives were in poor shape. What we needed, we could give each other.' He nodded. 'But that period's over now. I know it's over for me, and it's probably over for you, too. I mean, I've learned to live with it.'

'Go on.'

156

'What I'm trying to say is that . . . what I mean is that it wasn't love, Kenneth. It was a need, both physical and emotional, but never love.'

'I don't believe you.'

'I never lied to you. I never said I loved you.'

He stood up and paced the floor. Suddenly he turned. 'You wouldn't have said that before!'

'Before what?'

'Before he came.'

She rose, too. He did know! There was no use pretending. 'Leave him out of it!'

'You think I don't know what's been going on?'

'Nothing's been *going on*. At least, nothing that I'm ashamed of. Anyway, it's none of your business.'

'Of course it's my business! We were going out together. We were going to be married.'

'That was your idea. It was never mine.'

'You led me to believe . . .'

'If I did, I'm sorry.'

'When I talked about buying the house in Bonchurch and what we'd do . . .'

'You mean the golf? I didn't want to hurt you. I didn't want to take away your enjoyment.'

'My enjoyment! For Christ's sake, I wasn't just talking! I don't do that. When I want something, I get it. When I make plans, it's not just the making that's important, it's the fulfilling.'

'All right, Kenneth! If I gave you the impression that that was what I wanted, that that was what I was going to do with my life, then I'm sorry. I think you assumed too much. You assumed always that we'd get married. But we never really discussed it. You never actually asked me.'

He drew a deep breath and she saw that he was regrouping his thoughts. 'Look, let's not fight,' he said. 'I don't want to get into a row with you. I don't want this

157

to be the end of things for us. What's happening now is of no consequence. He'll go away and . . .'

'Stop saying that!'

'Face it,' he said. 'When he goes, you'll be lonely again, lonelier than you were before. You'll see.'

'Kenneth, it's not your business any longer.'

'It is.'

They stared at each other. 'I want you to go now,' she said.

'I've made it my business,' he said.

He turned and left the room. She heard him going down the stairs. She went to the window and watched him climb into the new shiny car. She expected a screaming of tyres, but he drove away smoothly. He must be more in command of himself than she was, she thought. She felt emotionally drained.

The uniformed Sergeant stopped in front of Bill and Sophie. He pointed down a short corridor. 'Second door on the right. Detective Sergeant Willis is waiting for you.'

They went into an institutional room with a scarred pine table and half a dozen straight-backed chairs. On the far side of the table, an open file in front of him, sat a round-faced man with thinning hair. He wore a tweed sports jacket and a heavy moustache that drooped, Zapata-like, on either side of his mouth. It gave him a rather forbidding look, but he smiled at them pleasantly and shook hands. They sat down.

'Now, sir . . .' He looked at the file in front of him. 'You've been in before, haven't you?'

Bill nodded.

'You saw Inspector Parker.' He steepled his fingers. 'You want to tell me about it, sir?' He snatched a quick glance at his watch. 'Just the facts, if you don't mind. My son's got a birthday party and . . .'

'Sure.' Bill sketched out the facts as he knew them, then prevailed upon Sophie, who had been sitting, stiff and silent, to tell her own story, up to her discovery of the used plastic bags and the empty glue-tubes.

Willis jotted down notes and when they had finished he said, 'I know those houses. I was born in Pimlico. Spent most of my life here, but the wife wanted trees and a bit of grass, so we moved to Bromley.'

Then he made them repeat the details of Miss Krause's death and Stefan's fall. At the end he said, 'You don't think he fell, do you, sir?'

'All I know is what the doctors told me,' Bill said. 'The injuries could have been made by blows.'

'I suppose that could be true of a lot of injuries. Take a car accident. You can never tell what injuries a person's going to sustain, but I'm sure some of them could be duplicated by blows. They are blows, in a way. Instead of something hitting the body, the body's hitting something.'

'I'm aware of that. We did find frozen milk on the pavement.'

'And on the steps,' Sophie said.

Willis looked at her expectantly and after a moment she said, 'Nobody takes milk. There was no broken glass.'

He made a note, then tapped his green Pentel on the desk top and said, 'What about these youngsters? Have you seen them since the car business?'

'No,' Bill said.

'And you haven't either?' he asked Sophie. She shook her head.

'Is there anyone with access to the houses, anyone who visits regularly, like?'

'Only Mr Ringham,' Sophie said. 'He collects the rents.'

'Ringham? I know that name . . .'

'A big man.' She looked at Bill. 'Like him. Wears an old-fashioned hat and a coat with a fur collar.'

159

'Got him!' Willis said. 'Ringham, Hubert. Of course! He set up as a rent collector when he came out.'

'Out of where?' Bill said.

'The Scrubs, I think. Might have been Pentonville.'

'Prison?'

'He did time for fraud. I think I'll have a word with Hubert Ringham, Esquire,' Willis said. He scratched his left wrist, easing up his shirt cuff, snatched another quick glance at his watch, then stood up. 'Well, thank you both for coming in.'

'What's the next step?' Bill said.

'We'll be round in the morning, sir. Have a good look over the houses. Take some fingerprints. See what's what.'

'Tomorrow morning?'

'That's a promise, sir.'

As he saw them out, he said to Sophie, 'I want you to ring us here, ma'am, if you hear anything, any noises, in the house. I'll leave a message with the Desk Sergeant. If I'm not here, someone else'll know about it. Don't just sit there, being afraid. Pick up the phone.'

She nodded and they walked out into the cold night air. Bill said, more to cheer her up than because he believed anything would be done, 'I guess that's got things moving.' He saw her into her flat and accepted her invitation to have a cup of tea. 'Tell me about this Mr Ringham,' he said. 'Does he live around here?'

Ronnie Flower drove over Battersea Bridge and into the Queenstown Road. A mist had settled on the river and the old power station loomed dark and brutish on his left. He drove to the borders of Wandsworth. The streets were mean, half industrialised, the houses were small and the council estates were large. Near the road to the heliport he turned into a maze of narrow streets comprising Victorian terraces. These were small villas, pleasant little houses when they had been built in the 1880s, but now the gardens had gone, tarred over to make hard-standing for cars. Railings had been broken down, walls had collapsed, hedges were unkempt and the roads were pot-holed. Ronnie drove carefully.

By comparison Sebastopol Square was heaven. This place would take years to come up – if it ever did – whereas the Crimea was on the move already. Soon Sebastopol Square would be hardly recognisable, all cleaned up. Well, they could keep it, Ronnie thought. He'd be sitting in the sun in his own ranch-style split-level house, and he'd have Denise. That's what he liked about her: she knew about nice things. He thought of the pink satiny bedroom. Real taste. No more corner shop, no more hairdressing salon. Everyone was the same in Spain. No class barriers there. If you had the money you were as good as anybody.

He drove along the miserable decaying streets until he came to a terrace where all the windows were boarded up. He knew they were due for demolition; another housing estate was going up here eventually.

He stopped, got out and made sure the car was locked. He hoped that when he came back the tyres would still be on it.

The first thing he heard was the music: a steady deep thud. He walked to the end of the terrace and entered a lane that ran behind the houses. There was a light shining dimly through the window of Number Three, and he knocked on the door.

'Yeah?' a voice called.

'It's me, Ronnie.'

The door was opened by a girl of about thirteen with bright orange and black hair. She did not look at him, did not greet him, but led him down a passage lit by a small gas-lamp. The paper had been stripped from the walls and electric wiring hung down like cobwebs. He had seen several squats in his time, but this was

161

one of the worst. It was freezing cold and smelled of lavatories.

He followed the girl into what had once been the downstairs drawing-room, the front room, the parlour of some neat Victorian family. Counting the girl who had led him in, there were six of them: the four boys and two girls. There were mattresses on the floor; magazines. A stereo with huge speakers blasted out sound.

Jack Jarvis was holding a joint carefully in his right hand. He took a drag and passed it on to one of the girls. Ronnie was almost afraid to touch anything in case some of their dirt and squalor rubbed off on him.

Jarvis said, 'Yeah?'

'I got a job for you,' Ronnie said.

'How much?'

'The usual.'

'Got any stuff?'

Ronnie put his hand into his coat pocket and brought out a dozen or more tubes of model aircraft glue and a roll of freezer-bags. He handed them to Jarvis.

The others stared at him as though he was less than human, perhaps not there at all.

'When?' Jarvis said.

'Tonight.'

Bill Seago stood outside Mr Ringham's flat in Inkerman Street and looked up at the first-floor windows. He'd rung the doorbell but there had been no reply. There was a light in the window, but most people left lights on when they went out these days. He banged on the door and a voice behind him said, 'You wanting Mr Ringham?'

He turned and saw the massive woman from the corner shop. She was regarding him from a few feet away.

'I guess he's out.'

'You been to his office?' Mrs Flower said.

'I was there a few minutes ago.'

'Sometimes he works late.'

'It's locked up.'

'Try The Bell. Down near the station. He likes a glass of stout about this time in the evening.' She gave him directions then rolled on down the street towards her shop.

She unlocked the door and was taking off her coat when someone tapped on the window.

'We're closed,' she called through the closed door.

A woman's voice said, 'I'm Denise.'

She opened the door and said again, 'We're closed.'

'I'm Denise.'

'Who?'

'Ronnie's Denise.'

'What about Ronald?'

'I'm his Denise.' She moved past Mrs Flower into the shop. 'I thought I'd just come round and meet you, since we never have, and since we're going to be family.'

'Family!'

'Well, by marriage.'

'I dunno what you're talking about.' Mrs Flower waved towards the door. 'I'm closed.'

Denise stared at her. A thought entered her head, and she decided to test it. 'Did he tell you about us? About the wedding? About Spain?'

Mrs Flower might have her problems with the written word, but her brain was perfectly capable of grasping the vernacular: words like 'wedding' and 'Spain'. She had heard them recently in the mouth of Hubert Ringham. Now she was hearing them again from this tarty looking creature who called herself Denise.

'He must've!' Denise said, in a voice that was meant to convince herself. 'Stands to reason.'

'Come with me,' Mrs Flower said.

163

Denise followed her up the stairs, past the boxes of model aeroplanes, to a room that was part store-room, part office, part dining-room. Mrs Flower indicated a chair at the table and Denise watched this mountain of flesh lower itself into another chair opposite her.

'Right, now,' Mrs Flower said. 'Just you pretend I don't know nothing at all.'

'But you *got* to know,' Denise said desperately. 'I mean, it's all arranged. The sale and everything. Even the home.'

'Home? What home would that be?'

'The one near Leatherhead. '*Course* you know! You're having me on. I mean, you signed the papers. Ronnie had them.' They faced each other in silence, then she said slowly, 'You mean, you didn't know, he never told you? Jesus! What a bloody bastard!'

'Start at the beginning,' Mrs Flower said. 'Like I told you. And don't call Ronald names, not in my house. I've never liked that sort of language. Anyway, if anyone calls him anything, it'll be me.'

Denise began to talk and soon she began to cry. Mrs Flower watched her in disgust and when she had finished, said, 'All right. You go home now.'

'What're you going to do?'

'That's my business.'

'I could sue, you know.' Denise sniffed angrily. 'Breach of promise.'

'Ever heard of conspiracy?' Mrs Flower said. 'You and Ronnie were conspiring to defraud me of my shop and to have me put away in a home. That's criminal, that is.'

'I never! It was Ronnie who said . . .'

'You start with the law and you'll be in trouble, my girl. Now go away.'

Mrs Flower sat at the table for a long while after Denise had left. She took down the box files of VAT returns and other papers. Everywhere she looked, she saw her signature.

He took advantage of me, she said to herself. My own son!

Maggie walked along one of the exposed corridors of Jamaica House, making for the stairway. She had just been to see Mrs Pocket. All the front doors were shut and she had the feeling that if anything happened to her, if she screamed, they would remain shut. In these buildings you kept to yourself. During the day when you went to work or did the shopping, you had to use the corridors and the lifts and the stairs, but they were no-man's-land, and you had to take your chances. When you got back, you locked yourself in and didn't come out unless you had to. She heard her own heels clicking on the concrete and hated the sound and tried to walk softly. Here but for the grace of God, she thought . . .

She went down the stairs clutching her medical bag as though it was a talisman. She came out into the orange lights and crossed the deserted walkways. She drove away from the estate into the heart of Pimlico, into its maze of streets, with real houses, where real people lived. And then she saw them.

They were walking in the direction of the 'Crimea', the four of them, one carrying the big silver ghetto-blaster. They were going away from her and she drew up at the kerb, wondering if Bill was at home. She hoped so. She suddenly thought of what might happen if he saw them or they saw him. She'd felt the anger in him after the beating. What if they did it again, and this time . . .? She tried not to think about it. Instead she cut down a side street and came out in Balaclava Place. She ran up the stairs of her house and as she did so she heard the telephone ringing in Bill's apartment. She stopped, waiting to hear him answer it. It went on and on until whoever it was decided that there was no one at home and gave up.

She knew he had gone to see Mrs Mendel, but that was a long time ago. Where was he now? Walking the streets, looking for them? And if he found them? She stood at the window, but all she could see was the empty street and the rows of parked cars.

Bill pushed open the door of The Bell and the stale beer and stale smoke hit him like a fist. It was a sad, formica pub, the kind of place small businessmen or middle management took their secretaries for a drink on the way to the station. There were half a dozen solitary drinkers in overcoats and hats having one for the journey home. The place was dead quiet.

The barmaid was in her early sixties, with dyed, gingerish hair and a thin lined face, heavily made up.

'I'm looking for a Mr Ringham,' Bill said. 'Mr Hubert Ringham.'

'You having a drink, dear?'

'I was wondering if you knew . . .'

'Sorry, I didn't hear.'

'Oh, all right,' Bill said. 'I'll have a Scotch.'

'Any particular kind?'

'Just as long as it's Scotch.'

'You did say a double, didn't you, dear?' she said, putting the glass in front of him. 'I know you American gentlemen like a real drink.'

The man nearest watched with a sour smile on his face.

'When do I get to ask the question?' Bill said.

'What was it you was wanting to know, dear?'

'I'm looking for Mr Hubert Ringham. I was told he came in here.'

'That's true enough. He does.'

'Have you seen him?'

'When?'

166

'Today.'

'Yes, dear.'

'When?'

'He left about twenty minutes ago.'

'You don't know where he was going?'

'No, dear, none of my business.'

Bill threw the whisky back into his throat.

'Thanks,' he said. 'Lovely place you've got here.'

As he reached the door the man with the sour smile said, 'Try The Duke. He often goes there.'

16

Mr Ringham had spent the early part of the evening in various Pimlico pubs. First he'd had a drink at The Bell, then two more at The Duke of Clarence, and finally he had dropped in at The Railway Arms. He now felt in the mood to face Ronnie Flower. He had to admit to himself that some of the gusto and verve he had felt when he had first spoken to Ronnie had vanished, leaving a rather empty feeling in his stomach. This needed to be overcome, for he *had* to remain in the driving seat. Everything depended on that. Now fortified, he not only felt that he *was* in the driving seat, but that he was capable of whipping up the horses as well.

As he approached Sebastopol Square, he saw that the shop lights were out, and of course Numbers Twelve and Fourteen were in darkness. There was no light even from Mrs Mendel's basement.

A figure materialised from between two parked cars.

'Evening, Ronald,' Mr Ringham said. 'Chilly, isn't it?' Ronnie did not reply. 'You might have picked somewhere warm.'

'You wanted safety. This is dead safe.'

'How's the fair Denise?'

Ronnie looked at him sourly, opened the door of Number Fourteen, and followed him in.

'What about lights?' Mr Ringham said.

'Do me a favour,' Ronnie said. 'There's no electricity. You should know that.' He lit a small gas-lamp that gave a strange white light, and they went up onto the first floor.

On the stairs, Mr Ringham sniffed and said, 'What's the smell?'

'I don't smell anything.' Ronnie opened the door of the first-floor flat and the smell was stronger.

Ringham said, 'Bring the light.' Then he saw that the door was closing behind him. 'What are you . . .?'

He felt their hands on him, dragging him forward. They were all over him like monkeys in a cage, clawing and tearing and kicking. He heard Ronnie's voice: 'It's a warning, Ringham. You keep out of my business.' He was dimly aware of a sickly odour, then a blow caught him in the face and he felt his teeth crack. Someone hit him on his right knee and he doubled up in pain. They were hitting him where they liked and he was bending, holding his arms around his head, trying to save his face, but they hit him on the neck, and the elbows. They were using short lengths of chain and galvanised piping. He knew they were killing him, but he couldn't stop them. He opened his mouth and tried to yell, but the sound that came out was like an old bull having its throat cut. A blow took him on the left side of the head which spun him round. He found himself falling . . . falling . . . and his brain seemed to explode.

Ronnie stood outside the door, listening. All he could hear was the thud and the crash and then the cry and the fall, and scraping thuds again and again and again. He opened the door and held up the light and saw Mr Ringham spreadeagled on the floor, and they were kicking him with their heavy Doc Martins.

'That's enough!' he shouted. 'Christ Almighty! Stop! Stop it!' He saw the blood and the green bile. 'For God's sake, what have you . . . oh, Jesus . . .!'

'You said do him proper,' Jarvis said.

'You've bloody killed him!' Ronnie's face was white and his eyes were wild.

'That's your look-out.'

One moment the boys were there, the next there was a drumming of boots on the stairs. The front door slammed and they were gone.

'Ringham!' Ronnie said. 'Ringham, can you hear me?'

He turned the body over. Ringham's dental plate was smashed in two pieces and lay on the floor beside his head. There was blood everywhere. 'Oh, Jesus,' Ronnie said again. He was trembling so much he had to put the lamp down.

One floor below and in the adjoining house, Mrs Mendel sat listening to the noise. There was nothing ghostly or supernatural, nothing at all other-worldly about what was happening. This was the noise of people fighting. The boys who sniffed the glue. She picked up her telephone and dialled the police, but in her anxiety her English deserted her and the man at the other end could hardly make out what she was saying.

'Glue?' he said. 'No, we don't have any glue.' She heard a laugh, as though whoever-it-was had half-covered the mouthpiece and was telling someone else. She thought of what he would be saying: some mad old woman.

'Give me your name,' the policeman said. 'That's what we must have first. Your name and address.'

She thought of Detective Sergeant Willis and the messages he said he would leave. He must have forgotten. His son was having a party. It was easy to forget.

'Can we just have your name, please?' the voice said.

She put the receiver down and cut the connection. She would try Stefan's son again. She had phoned him earlier, but there had been no reply. She wondered if he would be with the doctor; she had seen them together several

170

times. The noise continued above her, more loudly. She dialled Maggie Hollis's private number.

'He's not in,' Maggie said. 'Is there anything I can do?'

What could *she* do? Sophie thought. She wanted Stefan's son. She could trust him. He knew what they had seen.

She put the phone down without answering, leaving Maggie holding her receiver and talking into the air.

Ronnie put his head on Mr Ringham's chest, trying to hear his heartbeat, but his own heart was beating so loudly and his breathing was coming so quickly that the only sounds he could hear were those of his own body.

'Ringham! Ringham!' he whispered. But Mr Ringham did not move. Ronnie looked about in desperation. Ahead of him was a dingy kitchen that had not been used for a year or more. He searched for a receptacle, but could only see Mr Ringham's Homburg. He filled it at the cold tap with a rush of rusty water, and poured it on Mr Ringham's head. He didn't snap awake as they do in the movies, and as Ronnie had hoped. He lay quite still, a huge, collapsed hulk of a man, too heavy for Ronnie to move. Even if he could move him, the question was, where? Yet he couldn't be left where he was. If he could get him into the gardens . . . another mugging. Yeah, that was it. But how? He couldn't drag him down the stairs and across the street. Not without making a noise and probably being seen.

He placed the gas-lamp on the landing where it couldn't be seen from outside and went into the street. There was no time to return to the shop, so he hurried to the phone-box at the corner of the Square.

He dialled and after a moment he heard Kenneth Deacon's voice say in disbelief, 'Who?'

'Ronnie. Ronnie Flower.'

171

'I told you not to ring me at home. Not for any reason. Not ever.'

Ronnie said quickly. 'You'd better listen. Something important's come up, and it isn't good.'

'We had an agreement . . .'

'Don't give me that. I told you something's come up. I gotta have some help.'

'I might have known you'd never be able to handle your end.'

'I got a dead body,' Ronnie said.

'A what?'

'I said it was important.'

There was a pause and for a moment Ronnie thought he was going to ring off, then he said, 'Who?'

'It's Ringham.'

'Christ! What the hell's going on?'

'He found out.'

'About what?'

'About . . . about us. The houses.'

Kenneth's voice was suddenly calmer. 'How did he do that?'

'I dunno.'

'I think you do.'

'I swear to you . . .'

'Tell me what he knows.'

'What's it matter what he knows? He's dead! Listen, he's in Number Fourteen, on the first floor.'

'How did it happen?'

'The lads.'

'Why?'

'I told you, because he knew. It was going to be a warning, like. They went too far. We got to get him out of the house. Leave him in the gardens. Down by the old tennis hut. Make it look like a mugging.'

'Good idea. Why don't you do it?'

'Because I can't move him, that's why.'

172

'And you want me to come down there and . . . don't be daft!'

'Listen Deacon, this whole thing was your idea.'

'Accidents! For Christ's sake! *Accidents*. That was the idea.'

'We can still make it look like an accident.'

'Stop saying *we*! It's got nothing to do with me. You organised it, you fix it.'

'You bloody bastard!' Ronnie felt the sweat dripping down under his shirt front. 'You think I'd let you walk away and leave me? A couple of phone calls and you'd be up to your neck in it. You know what the coppers are like when they start to dig. I bet you got some other things you don't want across the front pages.'

There was another pause, but this time Ronnie knew Deacon wasn't going to hang up. 'All right,' he said. 'Stay where you are. I'll be with you in five minutes.'

Mr Ringham opened his eyes. He lay quite still, listening. Pain rolled over his body like swells at sea. Something deep inside him felt broken. Blood dripped from his nose, mouth and hair and mixed with the rusty water. Like some burrowing animal, in deadly fear of its life, he had lain doggo, making himself limp, like so much dead meat, until he'd heard Ronnie go down the stairs. Now terror gave his muscles strength. He knew he had to get away, but he could not stand without pain for his knee-cap was damaged. He began to drag himself towards the dimly lit doorway. On the landing he saw the lamp. Why had they left it? It could only mean they were coming back. He listened again. All was still. He knew these houses. He had known them since he was a child. There were rooms above, even attics. His mind, pressing for survival, seized on the fact that by leaving this room, causing them to search for him, he would gain time,

173

perhaps to recover his strength, to break a window, to pull himself towards the stairs, thinking to make for the room above. Then, in the dim lamplight, he noticed that the connecting door between the two houses was open. He crawled across the dusty floor, through the door, and closed it behind him.

Mrs Mendel heard the noise above her, a kind of slithering, as though someone was dragging a heavy parcel. She turned off her light and sat in the darkness in her chair near the sideboard. She was in the middle of her minefield. She followed the sounds until they disappeared towards the back of the house, and there was only silence.

Kenneth Deacon sat by the phone in the small study on the ground floor of his house in Prince's Square, looking sightlessly out of the window at the bare trees. From above, he could hear the faint sounds from Joan's new CD player.

Joan, the house, the business, Maggie, his ambitions, an expanding future in which he moved smoothly upwards – all were threatened. The one thing in his favour was that no one could connect him with anything that had occurred this evening, except Ronnie Flower.

He had always felt that Ronnie might be the weak link in his plans, but the chance to own a block of three houses on a corner site in an up-and-coming area of London had been too good to miss.

Ronnie hadn't been difficult to convince, and everything had gone smoothly, with one tenant after another being removed from the houses until only the old woman, Mendel, was left.

Then Ringham had entered the scene with his talk of a 'partnership', his insinuations to Joan about her grandfather, which he would have known she would pass on. But why had he suddenly changed tack and approached

Ronnie? Unless he'd seen him as an easier mark than Deacon, someone more susceptible to blackmail. And how had he found out what they were planning?

Well, it didn't matter. Ringham was dead and that saved Deacon having to do anything about him. There was only Ronnie now.

He unlocked the bottom right-hand drawer of his desk and from a yellow duster unfolded a small .22 pistol. He had bought it when he was on holiday in the United States and no one could trace it to him. It wasn't much of a weapon unless you were close to your target, but there was no reason why he should not get close to Ronnie. He stepped into the hall. Joan's music was still playing. He slipped out of the front door, closing it softly behind him.

Ten minutes after Sophie's call, Maggie realised she would not be able to relax until she had made sure that the old woman was not in trouble. She left a note for Bill and stuck it on her door.

It wasn't more than a couple of hundred yards from her house to Sophie's flat, but remembering the four skinheads she had seen earlier she decided to drive there.

The sound of her car entering the Square alerted Ronnie as he stood in the dark shadow of a plane-tree near the telephone-booth. Recognising the little Renault as the doctor's, he moved through a hole in the privet-hedge. He stood in the midst of a tangled shrubbery in the gardens and watched her. She found a parking place some distance down the road and walked back. She might be going anywhere. It didn't have to be – but then he saw it was. She went down the area steps of Number Twelve. To Mrs Mendel! He'd forgotten about the old woman in the basement. He thought of the noise of Ringham's beating in the house next door, the boots drumming on the stairs. That must be why the doctor had come: the fright could have given Mrs Mendel a turn. She'd tell the doctor what she'd heard. What then? Would Dr Hollis go into Number Fourteen to investigate? Would she call the police? Jesus, Ronnie thought, this place'll be like bloody Piccadilly Circus!

He couldn't go blundering in there with Deacon, not with the doctor wandering around.

His mind went back to his first meeting with Deacon. Ronnie had been having a quiet pint in The Duke when Deacon had come in. 'Course, it looked like a coincidence then, but now he could see that it had been planned. Planned right from the bloody word go. They'd got talking. Ronnie'd even been a bit flattered that Deacon had stopped to pass the time of day with him. They'd had another, and a third, and then gone onto shorts. Ronnie had always admired Deacon. He knew his old man had been in trouble – his mum had told him that – but Pimlico people didn't hold that against you.

Anyway, Deacon had put all that behind him. He'd married Edna, done well in his business – you only had to look around the streets to see his 'For Sale' boards – and Ronnie liked the way he dressed, not flash exactly, but you could see the money there. And the cars. Christ, he must have had one a year for the past few years: Alfas, a Mercedes, now the BMW.

They'd got talking about how you could make a pile out of property and how Ronnie and his mum were sitting on a gold-mine if they could only get their hands on the two houses next door as well. And he'd said, Well, his mum would never sell, so that was that.

And Deacon had said that was a pity 'cause it was such a good opportunity, like.

Ronnie hadn't slept that night. He'd met Denise by then and knew what he wanted: money and freedom.

The next time he had met Deacon was a few days later when his mum was at bingo. That was the time the lads came round for their supplies and he was just getting the stuff from the back when Deacon came in and the lads and Deacon stood there looking at each other and on the counter, in front of everybody, was the sign which said: 'We reserve the right not to sell solvents to any persons under eighteen'. And he could see that Deacon was looking at it and looking at the lads and thinking, Aye aye!

Ronnie wasn't sure when the actual decisive moment came. It seemed to him, thinking about it, that he'd just slipped into it. The papers his mum had signed, and putting the frighteners on the old people – that had been Deacon's idea. And when Ronnie had said how? Deacon had talked about young people and muggings and stuff like that and somehow Ronnie seemed to think of it all by himself. 'Use the lads!' he had said. 'We'll scare them out. Just accidents.'

And then that Miss Krause had dropped dead before the lads had even really started. They'd carried her into the gardens and made it look like a mugging, just to frighten the others.

Accidents! How the hell can you control an accident? Look what happened to the old chap. And now Deacon was blaming *him*!

He heard a crunch of gravel behind him. A shadow detached itself from the far side of the old tennis court and disappeared for a moment in the tangle of rhododendron bushes, then reappeared much closer to him. It moved without sound. It passed the side of the tennis hut. He lost it for a moment until it moved into the light from a street lamp, and he recognised Deacon. He was about to call when he saw the gun. Why a gun? Who was Deacon going to shoot? Ringham was already dead. And if it wasn't Ringham . . . The sweat

177

froze on Ronnie as he saw the trap he had nearly sprung.

Deacon paused in the shadows, examining the street,
then he put the gun in his pocket and stepped onto the
pavement. He looked into the phone-booth and crossed to
glance into the darkened shop of S. Flower and Son. Have
a good look, you bastard, Ronnie thought, you won't find
nothing there. He watched Deacon move back along the
opposite pavement, then push open the door of Number
Fourteen.

Ronnie ran across the road and let himself into the shop.

'Is that you, Ronald?'

'Yeah.'

He went upstairs. He was still sweating and frightened.
His mother was sitting at the dining-room table. She had
the box files down from the shelf and papers were spread
over the surface of the table.

'Sit down,' Mrs Flower said. 'You and me are going to
have a talk.'

It had taken Maggie several minutes to convince Sophie to
let her in. She stood marooned just inside the front door,
staring uncomprehendingly at the clutter on the floor,
frightened to move in case she tripped over something.
Sophie had returned to her seat at the table and looked
like some ancient sybil. The only light came from a small
lamp beside her.

'I came to make sure you were all right,' Maggie
said.

'*Ja*, I'm all right.'

'Have you been trying to phone Bill?'

'They said to phone if they eat the glue.' She pointed
towards the ceiling.

Maggie was thrown for a moment, then realised what
she meant. 'The boys have been there?'

Sophie nodded. 'And noise. Shouting.'

178

Maggie listened. 'It's quiet now.'

'Maybe. Maybe not.' She paused. 'I want Stefan's son. He knows.'

'I left a note for him. He should be back soon.'

Sophie did not reply. Maggie picked her way through the objects on the floor and sat at the table opposite her.

There was silence for some moments, then Sophie said, 'Do you believe houses can talk?'

'Talk?'

'Morris said it was the wood and iron. Expanding. Is that what you say?'

'Expanding and contracting.'

'I think it talks. I think it tells me things.' She broke off again.

To fill the silence, Maggie said, 'I see you're wearing the brooch.'

Sophie touched the Moroccan brooch. It was so heavy it pulled the front of her dress out of shape. She said, 'Leni had a brooch from her grandmother. Not so heavy like this one. They took it.'

'Who took it?'

'Those boys.'

Assuming her old mind had somehow muddled the skinheads with her daughter, Maggie decided that the time was rapidly approaching when Sophie would no longer be capable of living alone and looking after herself in this flat. She looked at the articles scattered on the floor, the narrow paths between them, the thick curtain that had been drawn over the window, shutting out any glow from the street-lamps. There was no doubt Sophie had deteriorated in the past few weeks. Her hair seemed lifeless, her face shrunken, her eyes farther back in her skull, yet they still burned brightly, like a bird's.

Sophie said, 'Listen!'

179

Her ears had picked up something out of place among the normal sounds of the house. She knew it so intimately now, all its creakings and groanings, its whisperings. That pattern had been broken by the lightest footfall on the boards next door.

Maggie began to move, but found herself suddenly in darkness as Sophie switched off the lamp. She heard the old woman's harsh whisper: 'You do nothing! You understand? Speak nothing!'

Deacon moved carefully up the stairs of Number Fourteen. Above him there was a faint glow from a gas-lamp on the landing. He brought the gun from his coat pocket, held it close to his thigh, out of sight, and called softly, 'Ronnie?'

The house was quiet. He wondered if Ronnie could be waiting for him in the darkness of the upper floor. But why? He couldn't be contemplating an attack, could he? Even if he suspected what he, Deacon, was planning, he wouldn't have the guts for that sort of thing. That's why he'd led him to think of those skinheads, the lads, he'd called them. 'My troops,' he'd said.

He slipped off the pistol's safety catch and entered the room, bracing himself for the sight of Ringham. But there was nothing except what looked like a pool of blood. He picked up the lamp and went through the flat. There were no signs of either Ringham or Ronnie. He examined the stairs that led down to the front door. There were no marks, no blood-spots. But back on the landing, he saw the trail leading away to the door which connected Number Fourteen with Number Twelve, next door. He put his hand on the door-knob. It was sticky with blood. He started back in disgust and cleaned his fingers with his handkerchief. Then, holding the gun in one hand and the lamp in the other, he went cautiously into Number Twelve. He followed the trail in the dust as

180

a hunter might follow a blood spoor. It led down to the darkness of the ground floor and stopped at a small door under the stairs.

The lamp was making plopping sounds as the little gas cylinder came near its end. But even in the fitful light he could see that this handle, too, was covered in blood.

Thinking that it must lead to a cellar, he tried the door. It was locked. He pushed against it. It was lightly made, with flimsy wooden panels. He raised his foot and smashed a hole in one of them, then he reached through and turned the key which was in the lock on the other side. He held up the flickering lamp and saw a narrow staircase descending to another door.

'Ringham!' he called. 'You there?'

As he reached the bottom stair, his lamp went out.

The two women sat in the darkness of the flat, listening.

'But surely that's . . .' Maggie whispered.

Sophie's fingers closed on her arm like talons. She winced in pain and closed her mouth.

The door opened and someone came into the kitchen, invisible in the total darkness.

Sophie heard a ringing note and knew that he was by the sink. Something dropped with a clang. Ladle, she thought. He's by the door.

Slowly her hand reached out for the little drawer in the sideboard.

A voice said, 'Ringham, I know you're in here.'

Maggie knew it was Kenneth, but she remained silent, still confused, bewildered by his presence, yet feeling his menace, his threat.

Sophie's old fingers searched in the drawer, but the space where the knife should have been was empty. Now she felt fear turn inside her.

Suddenly there was a crash. She knew what had happened: he had blundered into the birdcage and knocked it over. She heard him curse, then there was a fluttering of wings.

Now she remembered that she had dropped the knife somewhere upstairs. She had no weapon but the torch on her lap. If she moved to reach anything else, he would hear her. There was the chink of a teacup in its saucer. He was near the fireplace.

She put her hand up to her throat and felt the brooch. Silently she undid it, and held the long steel pin in front of her.

The room went silent. He's listening, too, Maggie thought.

'I know you're there, Ringham! I can hear you breathing.'

That's a lie, Sophie thought. Her ears were as good as anyone's. She couldn't hear breathing.

'Ringham!' It was a shout.

On the ground floor, near the back of the flat, Hubert Ringham heard his name. He was lying against a wall where he'd crawled after finding Mrs Mendel's door locked. Oh, Christ, he thought, they're coming for me again. He remembered the hands, the boots, the iron pipe. This time they'd kill him. He began to move to the front of the house.

Bill had asked for Hubert Ringham in The Bell, The Duke of Clarence and The Railway Arms, being passed from one to the next. There were also The Good Intent and The Jolly Sailor, but he decided that he'd had enough of looking for Mr Ringham. He could wait until the morning.

He had just come out of The Railway Arms near the big block of council housing along the river, and was turning into Balaclava Place when he saw the four skinheads crossing Inkerman Street, moving west. They were walking swiftly. He felt a surge of anger, a need for confrontation. At the same time, his mind urged caution. He had spent years in hostile and sometimes violent societies and had learned how to conduct himself. Instead of a confrontation, he decided to follow them. If he could find out where they lived, he would have some solid information for Sergeant Willis in the morning. The decision had taken only a fraction of a moment. Then, as he turned to follow them, another thought struck him. Their direction was taking them away from – Sebastopol Square! 'Oh, Jesus!' he said out loud, and began to run.

Sophie heard the tinkle of the wind chimes she had pinned up. He was near the curtain. She twisted in her chair to face that direction. There was the hollow clang of a saucepan being kicked. He wasn't more than a few feet from her and she inhaled the musk-like smell of his body and heard his breathing. Feet became inches. She snapped on the powerful torch, and his face was in front of her. She had only a second and in that moment she registered a familiarity. Then she saw the gun. As he aimed it towards the light, she stabbed forward. She had gone for his left eye, but he jerked instinctively and the brooch's long steel pin buried itself deeply into his nostril. He fell back with a cry. She put out the torch. He fired at the after-image.

On the pavement outside, Bill heard the shot. He raced down the area steps, shouting Sophie's name. The front door was locked. He picked up a heavy dustbin and smashed a gaping hole in the window. He climbed through, tearing at the heavy curtains, and light from the street poured into the room. A man was stumbling towards the bottom of the inner staircase. Bill saw him turn, heard the sound of a last random shot.

Hubert Ringham had pulled himself to his feet and was standing at the top of the little staircase. He saw Deacon below him.

In terror he cried, 'No!' as Deacon fired. He felt the bullet take him in the shoulder. His legs gave way. With another frightened bellow he toppled forward. Below him Deacon, already on the stairs, tried desperately to get clear. But it was too late. Ringham hit him with the force of a landslide. The two crashed to the floor, shaking the house, as Bill reached the women.

Sophie switched on the table-light. She was sitting exactly where she had sat all along.

Deacon lay, half-covered by Ringham, at the bottom of the stairs, his arm, with the pistol still in his hand, stretched out, his head at a strange angle to his shoulders. He was already dead when they dragged him free.

17

Maggie sat on the end of the bed and watched Bill pack. She had known this moment would come, had dreaded it and had tried not to think about it. He packed neatly. Practise, she thought, always travelling.

It was just after lunch on Sunday. They had gone out to a restaurant and she had drunk more wine than usual to help her get through the hours. His plane left at five and he had spent part of the morning with Sophie.

To fill the silence, she said, 'She's going to miss you.'

'Who?'

'Sophie Mendel.'

'She'll be all right.'

Nearly two weeks had passed since Deacon's death and Sophie had already moved into a new flat, small and light, with a view of the river. That very night, after the police and the ambulance had removed Deacon and Ringham, she had said, 'Now I go.'

'She's got one of the best views in London,' Bill said. 'She's perfectly happy there. She should have moved years ago. I guess I'll never understand her.'

'People were trying to force her out of her home. Things have to be on *her* terms.'

Maggie had hoped that he would be delayed, or at least have to return to London for Ronnie Flower's trial, but after the police had taken his statement they agreed that there wasn't anything more he could add. Ronnie had

185

signed a confession, it was said, and Ringham, in hospital, was unstoppable. He had even been able to identify the woman he had seen collecting letters from Deacon's mail-drop in Vauxhall Bridge Road as the secretary, Miss Marriner. 'When I saw Deacon at the bottom of the stairs, I knew,' he said dramatically. 'It was the last piece of the puzzle.' He and Detective Sergeant Willis had formed a cosy relationship, both being born and bred in Pimlico, and Ringham held a kind of court, propped up on his pillows, his face like boiled beef, his arm in a sling and heavy strapping around his ribs.

Bill and Maggie had heard most of the story when they were visiting him, and Willis happened to be there.

'It seems that Deacon, through his property company, secretly bought the two houses in Sebastopol Square a few years ago,' he said. 'As an estate agent, he knew it was on the way up – and he was right. He saw the chance to make a fortune if he could get his hands on the Flowers' house as well. Miss Marriner told us he'd already had plans drawn up to convert the three of them laterally into a luxury hotel.

'What hadn't occurred to him was that the remaining tenants in Numbers Twelve and Fourteen would flatly refuse to move out, even though he offered them money. That's why he and Ronnie Flower tried to frighten them into leaving. The idea probably came to him when Miss Oppenheimer broke her wrist falling off a bus. She deteriorated rapidly and had to go into care. Maria Krause was next. The young boys frightened her so badly she had a heart-attack, then they carried her into the garden and pinched her handbag.' He turned to Bill. 'Then your father died. He wasn't meant to die, just to fall. Hurt himself. Become scared of living alone. Still, if it hadn't been for you and Mrs Mendel, they might have got away with it. Nobody knew Mr Nedza had a son who might be suspicious about his death, and nobody realised just how tough the old lady is. She wasn't about to be frightened away from her home. So – there it is . . .'

Yes, there it was, Maggie thought, watching Bill slip his electric razor into one of his shoes.

He finished packing, zipped up the suiter, tied labels onto both it and his flight bag. There was nothing left to pack, nothing left to do.

'I hate goodbyes,' he said.

'So do I. I won't come to the airport.'

'No. I'll take the Underground.'

He held her for a long moment, then she said, 'Go now.'

He picked up his coat and two bags. As she stood at the window, she heard his footsteps going down the stairs for the last time. She watched him walk along Balaclava Place, a big man with a firm light stride. He didn't turn to wave and she was glad. Soon she would have to begin the process of erasing him from her memory, or at least, trying to. She looked towards Sebastopol Square, where it had all happened. 'For Sale' notices were just visible outside Numbers Twelve and Fourteen. When she turned, he had gone. The street was empty.

The days that followed were bare and bleak. They became weeks, a month, two months. The houses were sold and it was said they were going to be renovated as desirable residences. Ronnie Flower went to trial, pleaded guilty, and got five years. His mother visited him whenever she could, and it was said that her visits left him extremely depressed and nervous. The four young skinheads, none older than fourteen, were scooped up from their Wandsworth squat and punished with what the Government described as a short, sharp shock. Mr Ringham recovered and was seen again on the streets, thinner, but retaining his old bravado. In The Bell or The Duke he always had a good audience for what became a kind of one-man show: how Hubert Ringham solved the Sebastopol Square killings.

These were the marking stones in the weeks after Bill's departure. For the rest, Maggie tried to bury herself in her work. She had decided to go to Florence on a culture holiday, and prepared herself by reading the lives of Raphael, Botticelli and Andrea del Sarto and discovering finally who the Guelphs and who the Ghibellines were. She gave herself little time to brood.

She often saw Sophie, with whom she had struck up a friendship. Sometimes they spoke of Bill, though Sophie never called him that. She always referred to him simply as Stefan's son. This pleased Maggie, because it turned him into another person. As Maggie drank tea and ate damp biscuits, Sophie's mind turned more and more frequently to her childhood visits to Lübeck with her father. She was still stubborn and tough, but in the past weeks some of the fire, Maggie thought, had gone. Who could wonder? So, apart from friendship, Maggie also kept a watchful medical eye on her.

One Saturday afternoon, Sophie telephoned her. Her voice sounded strange, so Maggie hurried round to see her. It was a warm, spring day. As she turned along the Embankment, the sun flashed on the Thames like fire.

Sophie's flat was in a low-rise building, built to human scale. Maggie rang the doorbell, apprehensive that something had happened to the old woman, that this was the beginning of her end.

Bill opened the door. He stood, bigger than she had remembered, blocking out the light. Her surprise was complete. She could not speak.

'I was passing through London,' he said.

Suddenly she was angry. 'God damn you! I was just getting over you!'

He looked at her solemnly. 'I'm sorry. I thought we could meet as friends.'

She followed him into the flat. 'Where's Sophie? She phoned me.'

'I know. I asked her to.'

'I hate practical jokes!'

'So do I.'

'Where is she?'

'She's shopping. She's fine.'

'Then I must go. This isn't . . .'

'Give me a minute. I thought we might have dinner tonight . . .'

'No.'

'. . . and then tomorrow we can talk . . .'

'I don't want to . . .'

'. . . about the future.'

'I'm not going through any more . . . what *future*?'

'*Our* future.'

'We don't have a future, remember?'

'What would you say to Australia?'

She was still angry. 'The phrase "hello Australia" springs to mind. What would you?'

'I mean to live. You and me. In holy wedlock.'

She stared at him. 'Are you serious?'

'Dead serious. I've been offered a contract there. You could practise. I've checked. If you say "yes", I take it. If you say "no", I go to the Southern Sudan for three years. You can't seriously do that to me.'

'You're a bastard! What if I'd been away? And I'm about to go to Florence.'

'I know all that.'

'How?'

Sophie Mendel came in. 'You had enough time,' she said. 'Now I make tea. You celebrating something? You want a glass of port?'

Bill looked at Maggie. She said, 'Yes, we're celebrating something, but tea will be fine. For the moment.'

189

If you have enjoyed this book and would like to receive details of other Walker mystery titles, please write to

Mystery Editor
Walker and Company
720 Fifth Avenue
New York, NY 10019